M000236814

Advance Praise

"Karl Dehmelt's *The Theory of Talking to Trees* is simultaneously subtle and powerful. Stephen Christiansen and Isaac Sellers are two men whose lives are each touched by mental illness. Dehmelt crafts their story in such a way that the reader is aware that each man's life has been impacted profoundly by mental illness, but the minute details lurk just off the edges of the pages. It is this dance between the known and the unknown that humanizes *The Theory of Talking to Trees* in a profound way. The story connects reader and characters in a way that has the reader embracing the characters long after the last page has been turned."

   —Tanya J. Peterson, author of *Twenty-Four Shadows*
      and other novels about mental illness

"Writing is a lonely process, and every now and then you come across a book that perfectly captures that experience. *The Theory of Talking to Trees* is one of those books. It's rare to find someone with whom you want to share the writing experience and, as Karl Dehmelt tells us, it's also very fragile."

   —Wes Peters, author of *Between the Doors*

"Dehmelt's second novel, set in Baltimore and full of local color, is packed with cinematic action. Stephen, an aspiring novelist, and Isaac, a veteran of mental illness and homelessness, survive a mugging together and become friends. The two share hopes, fears, dreams and heartbreaks until the final tragedy in this vigorous, readable pageturner. The promising young author is certainly one to watch."

—Ellen Prentiss Campbell, author of *The Bowl with Gold Seams*

"*The Theory of Talking to Trees* attacks the topic of mental illness with fearlessness and honesty and with the speed of a car barreling down the Jones Falls Expressway at dawn. This book's a page turner, as moving as it is thrilling, and is truly a Baltimore novel through and through. With an excellent 'sophomore' novel, Karl Dehmelt has arrived on the scene."

—Lucas Southworth, author of *Everyone Here Has a Gun*
Professor at Loyola University Maryland

The Theory of Talking to Trees

Karl Dehmelt

The Theory of Talking to Trees

Karl Dehmelt

Apprentice House
Loyola University Maryland
Baltimore, Maryland

Copyright © 2016 by Karl Dehmelt.

All rights reserved. No part of this book may be reproduced or transmitted in any form or by any means, electronic or mechanical, including photocopy, recording, or any information storage and retrieval system, without prior permission from the publisher (except by reviewers who may quote brief passages).

First Edition

Printed in the United States of America

Paperback ISBN: 978-1-62720-121-6
E-book ISBN: 978-1-62720-122-3

978-1-62720-121-6

Design: Luisa Beguiristain
Editorial Development: Caroline Tell

Published by Apprentice House

Apprentice House
Loyola University Maryland
4501 N. Charles Street
Baltimore, MD 21210
410.617.5265 • 410.617.2198 (fax)
www.ApprenticeHouse.com
info@ApprenticeHouse.com

To Nate.

PART I

[1]

The sirens which rang in the night fade in the morning.

Stephen Christiansen closes the door carefully, and ensures it's locked. While he hasn't heard of any recent robberies in the area, it's better to be safe than sorry. He returns the keys to the pocket of his sleek black suit jacket. His shoes clack on the pavement as the hems of his dress pants skirt his heels. A dark blue tie rests lazily on his chest, perfect for the chilly feistiness of the September morning. Phoebe had left twenty minutes ago; he places the trash in the tall garbage bin, remembering how she'd pounced on him earlier.

"Were you dreaming about me again?" she'd asked, lying beside him in their bed.

He'd said no then; now, he squints, attempting to block the returning rush of what had woken him in a cold sweat.

There's a knoll nestled into the side of a hill, covered with emerald grass. She sits amongst the blades, her strawberry hair cascading down her shoulders. She's a stranger, but also the love of his life. A thousand birds circle overhead, tracing patterns like a paintbrush. In her blouse of striking teal, she's prettier than any model, yet simple in her grace. Treading through the field, his fingers whish over the plain and it bends.

She is fading.

The closer he walks, the more the radiance seems to drain from her face, as if she's waking up the morning after a funeral. He reaches out a hand, clasping the air, a child lost in a grocery store. The caressing of the wind turns abusive. Above, the birds fly off into the distance. A wrathful pack of thunderclouds now sail on the turning skies.

Her smile morphs into pain. His feet slog in the trenches of the earth, each leg resisting the pull of his muscles and drenching him in the fats of the land. The ground slopes upward, and she's standing above him. He trips and stumbles, attempting to climb the sudden parapet between them. She covers her mouth with a porcelain hand, her eyelashes catching tears. Her gaze moves to him, and his hands claw at the shaking dirt.

His calls to her are lost to the elements. Fighting to get closer, he keeps reaching, his veins infused with adrenaline. His muscles lock. She shakes upon the top of the hill; her hair is now matted upon her cheeks. Squinting through the storm, she backs away across the top of the mound towards an edge, shaking her head violently.

At last, he reaches the top of the mountain, stretching his hand out to her. His arm caked with mud and water, he can see her slowly falling.

A word cuts through the storm as she tumbles into the ether on the opposite side of the hill:

"One."

With that whispered word, he'd snapped to life with a jolt, his neck sore and pulse racing.

An ambulance drives silently down the street in the distance.

Walking to his car, Stephen hits the key fob twice. The 2012 Yaris has weathered the snows and rains of the past two years; granted, it's only sustained one winter thus far, with the ice of 2015 waiting to burst the car's windows and shank its tires. Stephen walks to the driver's side door with Phoebe on his mind.

The drive to Baltimore's Bessemer Press is only ten minutes from Carbondale's humble brick apartments. Phoebe's route to Sinai Hospital is even shorter, only seven minutes.

She'd asked if he loved anybody else the same way he loved her, and he'd said no.

"Not even the adoring bimbos who tattoo your name all over their boobs?" she'd asked. He'd assured her that she's the only girl he'd ever dream about.

"Oh, my hero!" she'd batted her eyelids. "Does that mean you'll take out the trash when you go to work?"

As he sits behind the wheel of the Yaris, he looks over to the passenger seat to examine the stack of pages adorning the fine cloth. He'd placed them there so he'd remember his job after the weekend. While many in the editorial business prefer to use computers as their means of correction, Stephen's always preferred to review by hand. He takes each manuscript assigned to him, whether it's for a blockbuster, rollicking action novel; a reserved, dignified memoir; or a sexually deviant romp, and reads them aloud. His boss, the honorable Mr. Charles Leonard Don't-You-Miss-One-Fucking-Error Shultz, originally balked at the premise of Stephen using his own free-time to parrot the entirety of manuscripts vocally. Instead of his anger being meant as a slight to his process, Shultz had loved the idea, but then plaintively asked exactly what Stephen did during the days on company time, to which Stephen simply smiled.

"I work the same way at home as I do when I'm in the office!" Stephen had said.

"Don't you think it's important to take some time off? To go and maybe leave work behind, if only for a little bit, so you don't stroke out one day screaming about the passive voice?" Shultz had asked.

The car coasts to a stop at the end of the street.

Shultz doesn't appreciate the source of Stephen's motivation. When his parents used to beat the shit out of each other over his father stealing money from his mother, he'd worked. After his mom had been diagnosed with inoperable cancer, 15-year-old Stephen had read stories in the hospital lobby, his mind becoming tuned to detect mistakes like a concert pianist at the keys. He'd been reading a copy of Tim O'Brien's *The Things They Carried* when his mother passed.

Only five minutes through the commute, the car waits at another stoplight. Reaching into a niche next to him, he pulls out a carton of cigarettes. He'd stopped smoking back in 2010, a habit which he'd broken at Phoebe's urging. The thought of *The Things They Carried*, Stephen muses, allows him to stop and consider all he'd left behind. Thinking better of his refractory impulse, he drops the smooth white of the cigarette pack down onto the center console, and flicks on the radio to hear the morning news.

Eventually, the wall of traffic breaks into a free flow. Stephen taps his fingers on the side of the steering wheel; he hears about how the Orioles might finally break out of the perpetual sadness factory of recent losing seasons. The landmarks which define a location eventually seep into a resident's bloodstream like a well-intentioned infection, eating up their free time graciously. Stephen refers to abundances of un-used time as the *dead periods* of the day, which he's minimized since he learned the value to be found in living.

[2]

At his desk, Stephen is the lord of corrections. A copy of his latest novel, *Calls to a Crowded Room*, sits next to his computer, its cover glossy and reflective. The novel details how a young teenager is injured in a nearly fatal car accident, and his family is left to bring him back to health through endless hours spent in the emergency room. They scrape the morsels of optimism from a full plate of tragedy, fearing the young man might not awaken from his comatose state. The title refers to how the protagonist, a friend of the injured boy, remembers the family sitting in isolation in the intensive care unit of the novel's hospital with nothing but condensed concern and endless phone calls.

"Good morning, Stephen!" a voice chimes from outside the office door.

A man pokes his head around the corner; a beard, a mix of brown and gray, tightly outlines his chin. His woodsy eyes flash with a sparkle.

"Good morning, Director Shultz," Stephen rises from his desk, his fingers tracing the aged mahogany.

"How are you on this fine morning? I see you've re-discovered your love of your own work!" Shultz gestures to the copy of *Calls to a Crowded Room* on Stephen's desk.

"Yup, it truly is a love-hate relationship."

"*Calls to a Crowded Room* ... hmmmmm," Shultz's hand strokes the hair on his chin, one eyebrow raised. "You know where you should call if you don't want a crowded room?"

"Where?"

"Your book signings."

"Thanks, Charles."

"Hey," Shultz grins, mockingly apologetic. "I'm always here to give you direction, which is why I am called the director." He outlines a nametag pinned to the lapel of his suit jacket.

"So I must be the editor because I correct all your errors, right?" Stephen jabs.

"See, it's a complex relationship. If you and I were a Facebook couple, I'd change our relationship status to 'it's complicated', less because of our professional exchanges and more because I would love to …" Shultz coughs. "Uhm, what's the proper term for it? I'd like to take your fiancée on a nice date!"

"What does Jen think about that?"

"She agrees. She would also like to take Phoebe on a nice date."

"How does Wednesday night sound?"

"Perfect!"

"Can I come?"

"Maybe if you finish the batch of edits for the manuscript I gave you three weeks ago instead of re-reading your own novels. God knows you have enough since nobody buys them," Shultz says.

Considering the offer, Stephen's guise is quizzical.

"That's a difficult decision," Stephen says. He walks back to his desk, and leafs through the stack of papers which he'd brought with him to work.

"Oh, well would you look at that! You actually finished them ahead of schedule!" Shultz's voice is a cocktail of sarcasm.

"Amazing, right? I figured you would've learned—back at UMD when we were roommates and you tried to carry a steaming hot batch of popcorn in a Ziploc bag, causing it to melt all over the floor of our room—that the less time I spend dealing with your shit, the better." Stephen says.

A true laugh emerges from behind Shultz's placard of chuckles.

"You don't forget anything, do you?" Shultz takes the first half of the papers from Stephen.

"Nope, and you should know that by now."

"Christ," Shultz looks them over quickly; the pages are bleeding with marks from a red pen. "Did that popcorn incident happen before or after you and Phoebe started dating?"

"It was back when you still wanted to call this place 'TreeSpring Press', before you even had the job."

"Listen, kid," Shultz finishes his flipping. "If you're going to dream of taking over a publishing company, you have to shoot for the stars. I told you I'd have it all accomplished by the age of 26, now look at us—we're both 28, I'm the director, and you have travelled with me as my ever-present assistant. You are truly the Robin to my Batman!"

Rolling his eyes at Shultz, Stephen clicks his pen.

"I'm not going to dress in a skin-tight suit so you can admire me more than you already do."

"Admire you?" Shultz walks to Stephen's desk. "Why would I admire you? You've only gotten three books published since the age of 22, and still nobody outside of Baltimore gives a shit who you are, and no, your family doesn't count—not because they're your family, but because they don't give a shit, either."

"Well, nobody knows who you are outside of these Bessemer offices, so I think I'm a little more socially connected than you are, oh Mr. Supreme Galactic Commander," Stephen retorts.

"Not yet!" Shultz says, picking up a pen from Stephen's desk. "If my plans go to fruition, however, and we start publishing books which are a little more developed than the amateur shit you keep writing, then we'll be big in no time!"

"Oh, right, because of 'networking'. I'm sure you've brown nosed enough by now that you'll be ready for the big time deals when they come our way," Stephen clicks a pen on the side of the desk.

"At least I've been cozying up to others; you've been infatuated with yourself."

"Touché."

The two pause, grinning.

"In seriousness, how are the numbers looking?" Stephen asks.

"Good, very good. If *Calls* keeps trending the way it is, we have an outside shot at the *Times'* Bestsellers list."

At the mention of the commercialist's Holy Grail, Stephen's mouth gapes in reverence.

"Are you serious?"

"Yeah. The bumps in our media here, plus that interview you did last weekend with the *Sun*, really helped. Alternatively, we could both sell our homes so that you could buy a thousand copies of your own book in bulk, which would allow us to sit together at our offices here, completely out of luck, but it would feel good to see 'Stephen Christiansen: *New York Times* bestselling author', wouldn't it?"

"I can't believe it," Stephen scoffs.

"Neither can I."

Striding to stand behind Stephen, Shultz claps him on the shoulder.

"We made it, kid." Shultz says.

"No, you made it. This entire publishing idea was your brainchild since junior year."

"Yup, and we needed writers like you to do it. Do you remember what an atrocity this place was when we got here?"

"Yeah, there were mice everywhere and hungry writers prowling the office isles."

"Not quite," Shultz says with a laugh. "But it was bad, it was real bad. All it took was two crazy bastards with a dream and degrees in Business and English, right?"

"It doesn't take a degree to be a writer. The people make the degrees, the degrees don't make the people."

"Oh, cut me a break," Shultz says with a pained expression. "Save it for your acceptance speeches."

They break their half-embrace as Shultz turns to leave.

"What?" Stephen calls after him. "No 'thanks for getting this in early, Steve?' Nothing?"

Already in the doorframe, Shultz turns around.

"You know what I've realized since we've done this together? It's really quite profound." Shultz says.

"What?" Stephen asks.

"You're a prick."

Stephen winks.

"Right back at you, Charlie."

[3]

Walking out of the Bessemer building, Stephen lets the door close behind him. The glass reverberates in the center of the wooden frame, the golden 340 stenciled at the top glinting in the descending sun. Stephen's mind drifts, base-jumping the highs and lows of the past month. The news of his sales this morning signifies he's starting to transition from being a big fish in a small pond to a hungry guppy in a lake. His car is parked in the shadow of the foreboding stone of the Bessemer offices.

Rounding the corner of the sidewalk, Stephen steps over cracks filled with small weeds. The streets are usually slow at this time of day, with the townsfolk nestled indoors. A few townhouses outside his price range fill the buildings on each side of the street, with a nice park a few miles away. The urban section of Baltimore seems a little apprehensive today, almost like it's holding its breath.

As he looks down the street, Stephen understands why.

Three men stand about ten feet in front of him. They're next to a car of cherry red and a porch which leads to a dilapidated building. Two of the men are facing away from him, and their backs grow closer as Stephen takes two steps towards them, even as his mind screams for him to stop. Sweat forms on the inside of his shirt, down his arms, and around the circle of his neck.

The man standing on the right is dressed in a thick leather jacket.

His jeans are equally black, baking under the waning sun. His hair is suppressed by a gray beanie, folded tightly. The gloves on his hands cause Stephen's mind to conjure up a history for this character in front of him, perhaps one involving a rap sheet miles long. On the left, the *amigo* of Stephen's new antagonist stands a head shorter than the man in the leather jacket. He too wears a coat, except his more fits to the form of a mannequin displaying the latest trends in a department store. His hair is tightly cropped and a sleek brown. The man's pale skin is much different than the dark tone of the first man; Stephen dimly notes the successful integration of two races in the plotline he's forming beneath the part of his brain that is yelling for him to

TURN AROUND AND RUN THE OTHER FUCKING DIRECTION.

Two earrings descend down the sides of the man's face, with two sizeable gauges carved into his ear lobes like hanging moons in cloudless sky. The red of his jacket traces the sides of his body to two hands adorned with rings. Stephen's feet finally obey his mind and stop, and as his body jolts to a sudden halt, Stephen spies the third man, whose face is barely visible beyond the other two figures.

He's wearing glasses like Stephen used to wear in high school. Stephen sees his nicely collared shirt of baroque white off-setting his brown skin. He's the same complexion as Mr. Leather on the right, and markedly darker than Mr. Gauge on the left. His eyes dart between the two men in front of him, whose faces Stephen cannot see; the man's hands hover awkwardly near the pockets of his deep blue jeans. His sneakers point forward reluctantly, ready to turn around and dash at the nearest chance. Stephen stands separate from the scene as if he's a God returned to earth, observing his creations.

"Isaac, I knew just from looking at you we were meant to be friends," Mr. Gauge's voice ricochets back to Stephen, whose heart accelerates in his chest. Gauge's ratty tone eclipses two rows of yellowed teeth.

"I told you guys, I don't want any trouble," The man—Isaac,

presumably—puts up both hands with his palms open.

"We don't want any trouble either, Ike. Consider this a business exchange." Mr. Gauge spits onto the sidewalk, tobacco residue bobbing in the bead of white.

"I already gave you my wallet. You guys can have all the money in it, you can take all my credit cards and I won't cancel them."

"Yeesh," Mr. Gauge snorts. "That's very generous of you. But we both know that as soon as you get home you're going to cancel everything you own, and then we'll be left with plastic cards. They do me no good if I can only divide lines on them, they're worth a lot more if they actually buy shit."

"No, I swear," Isaac says, stepping back from the pair, his voice steady to compensate his wavering expression. "I won't cancel the accounts. All the transactions you make I'll approve if you let me get out of here."

Mr. Leather snorts, but remains still.

"I don't believe you, Isaac. I've watched you come and go from your house for a while, and I know you're lying to us," Gauge's rings rattle as he brushes the right side of his coat.

Putting his hands down, Isaac flicks his fingers across his palms, slick with sweat.

"Why would you lie to us?" Gauge leans into him. "We never did anything to you. We're two guys looking to make a living, you know? We're out here taking back what is rightfully ours, which has been denied to us thanks to the system. Now, while I wish we could collect our comeuppance from *anybody* else but you, I know this is going to turn out better for you if you open the car and give us what you were putting inside."

Isaac's eyes flash to the passenger side door of the car, the reddened, rusted 2004 Cadillac sedan. A small white bag sits on the seat, displaying the good tidings from the local pharmacy, declaring *thank you for shopping at Baltimore Pharmaceuticals!* His left hand twitches towards the door momentarily before returning to his side.

"What's wrong?" Gauge asks, tilting his head sideways, the metal in his ear jingling like a chime.

"Those cost a lot of money, man," Isaac says.

"Oh really?" Gauge steps back, his eyes widening. He turns to Mr. Leather. "You hear that, Joey? Those pills cost a lot of money!"

Mr. Leather smiles, his breath mixing with the tepid air.

"Please," Isaac says, his voice dropping. "If you take my medicine, I won't be able to feed myself and my wife."

"Oh, you have a nice looking wife, alright." Gauge snickers. He turns to Mr. Leather and taps him on the shoulder. "You know what my favorite part about Ike here is?"

"What's that?" Leather asks.

"He talks like a white boy," Gauge says.

"Please, I'm begging you," Isaac's voice wavers, "don't take my pills. I'll give you anything else. I won't cancel the cards, I'll give you the shirt off of my back-"

"Listen here," Mr. Leather snaps. His smile has been replaced by a rough expression. "You dirty, bottom feeding, fuckin' piece of trash. If you don't open up that fuckin' door right now and give me those pills, I'm going to send your worthless ass back to your bitch dissected in a motherfuckin' trash bag."

The force of the statement causes Isaac's pupils to dilate, as if being filled by black water. Mr. Gauge cracks a laugh under his breath.

"Dammit, Isaac. You've gone and pissed off Joey. Joey doesn't like it when our clients aren't cooperative. While they usually say the customer's always right, in this case you're fucked, bucko."

Lowering his head, Isaac resigns himself to his position as prey.

"What kind of pills you got in there?" Gauge asks, Isaac's wallet open in his hands. His stick fingers flip dollar bills, counting silently.

"Clozapine." Isaac mutters through quick, jabbed breaths.

"Really?" Gauge stops counting. "How much?"

"A month's worth."

"Holy shit, you really are psychotic," Gauge taps Joey on the shoulder lightly, his laughs echoing through the empty street. Nobody's come to see the scene; residents know which streets to avoid.

"That's what I said, isn't it?" Leather laughs, stroking his jagged stubble. "He's completely out of whack, fucked up in the head. You should've downed those capsules all at once, you piece of shit. Would've probably done your girl some go-"

"Hey."

A new voice splits the air. Gauge stops counting and wheels around. Leather turns slowly, his face expressionless.

Like a man awaiting execution, Stephen's chest is tight and his tone is defiant.

"What the fuck do you guys think you're doing?" Stephen asks.

"Walk along," Gauge says, continuing to count.

Stephen doesn't move.

"I said walk along, motherfucker, this is none of your business! Didn't anybody teach you manners?" Gauge raises his voice, the bills in his hand.

"Yeah, people taught me to treat others like I'd want to be treated."

"Amazing," Gauge says, storing the money in his pocket. "Then how about you stop interrupting shit you know nothing about, and keep walking?"

"You know that man?" Stephen asks, gesturing to Isaac in the background.

"It's none of your business who or who we don't know, you retarded honky," Leather takes a step towards Stephen, his jacket puffing in anger. "And if you keep raising your voice and talking shit to us, it's going to become your business, and you don't want to fuckin' do business with people like us."

"Wow, that's original," Stephen says, chortling a tad. "People like you disgust me."

"Yeah, and dumbasses with no manners disgust me too," Gauge's voice is armed. "Stay where you are," Gauge says to Isaac, who's leaning up against his car, watching Stephen with a nauseated expression.

"Again, extremely original," Stephen says. "I didn't know Aaron Hernandez got traded to the Ravens and then started walking around Baltimore robbing people."

"Oh, so you're funny *and* stupid?" Leather says to him. The two stop advancing on Stephen, and Leather reaches into the inside of his jacket. A shiny piece of black metal glints on his hip, and Stephen's blood suddenly lags in his veins.

"Walk away now, or I'm gonna turn you into a pincushion, white boy," Leather growls.

Looking past them, Stephen sees Isaac issuing a silent apology.

"Three seconds," Leather says, removing the .45 from its holster. "Two."

His throat coarse, Stephen swallows, but the action seems futile.

Gauge slams against the stone wall of the building, Isaac's weight plowing him into the slabs as Isaac rips one of his earrings straight through the lobe. Blood sprinkles the pavement of the sidewalk below as Gauge lets out a shocked scream of fury and surprise. Leather turns around at the sound, and Stephen kicks in him the back of his knees, causing him to stumble forward. Gauge and Isaac grapple near the wall as a siren wails in the distance. Stephen punches Leather once in the side of the head, but then finds himself spinning backwards after an elbow catches him in the stomach.

Leather is quick to his feet. The .45 shines hungrily as the sirens grow louder. Stephen clutches his side, and the world seizes into slow motion.

The safety clicks, and Leather pulls the trigger.

The bullet exits the barrel in a blinding flash, and Stephen staggers backwards, clutching his left shoulder as the shot eviscerates his suit jacket and sends him spiraling.

Pain sears through Stephen's body from the hole in his shoulder as his vision blurs. He barely sees Isaac drop Gauge's body to the ground, where Gauge crumples, blood spewing from his mouth and the remnants of his ear. Isaac knocks the gun out of Leather's hand, sending it skidding on the sidewalk. The scream of the siren overwhelms as Leather strikes Isaac, knocking him to the pavement.

Through the shock, Stephen gasps; as impending orders for Leather to drop to the ground fly around his ears, Leather's fist hurtles towards his head, rocketing into the right side of his skull.

[4]

Curtains, the color of illuminated cherry blossoms, flutter gently. The breeze kisses the side of Stephen's face as he's thrust into artificial light. His crusty eyelids shutter twice, his eyeballs peeking. Moving his head to the left, his neck cries out in protest as he manages a cough. Feeling returns to him like a wave on a receding shoreline. As his vision focuses, he sees Phoebe shifting into view.

"Hey there," Phoebe says. Her smile is vapid.

"Hi," Stephen murmurs. He shifts on his pillow, but his left shoulder refuses to comply. Soreness seeps from his wound like a wildfire, arching through his arm, forcing his teeth into a grimace.

"So this is what happens when I let you go out alone?" Phoebe's voice wavers.

"Yeah," Stephen replies, the tempest of pain fading. His breathing slows.

"If they'd brought you to Sinai and I'd seen you rolled in on some stretcher, I would've probably dropped dead on the spot," A tear wets Phoebe's dimples.

"I'm so sorry, Phoebe," he coughs, his shoulder bouncing in its socket.

"I'm glad you're alright," She squeezes his hand, and her touch calms him.

"Where are we?" he asks.

"We're at Hopkins. It was the closest to Bessemer's building," She reaches into the pocket of her blue jacket.

"What the hell time is it, even?" Stephen asks. He tries to move his head further to the right, but his skull feels numb. The left side of him feels the breeze, but the crown of his head on the right side seems askew.

"It's nearly nine. Your surgeries bogged down the schedule."

"My what?"

"Your surgeries, dumbass," Phoebe traces his fingers with her own.

"Why did I need surgery?"

"You got shot."

The words skirt around Stephen's head like buzzing insects.

"I got shot? By who?"

"Me, of course," Phoebe says,

"Funny. What happened?"

"The police said you're one of the luckiest shooting victims they've ever encountered. You were shot at close range by a .45 cal, and then you got the shit knocked out of you by a blow to the right side of your head."

A faded leather jacket dances on the edge of Stephen's memory; a man with gauges. The flash of the muzzle explodes in the creative center of his mind, as if he's writing the scene in a story.

"The bullet entered your shoulder and missed the brachial artery, along with the subclavian, and it also managed to only graze a part of the bone. Basically, it shot right through you. If it'd been a couple more inches in either direction, it would've struck something important, and I would've lost you," Phoebe's years as a nurse hold her tears at bay.

Flexing his hands, Stephen looks down to the large bandage covering his shoulder – right beyond the tubes snaking out of his nose.

A couple more inches in either direction, and I'd be dead.

The bed underneath him seems to spin, loose on its foundation. He looks back to Phoebe, who continues clutching his hand, the engagement ring on her finger blinking dutifully. She's smiling now, gratitude radiating from the wounded look in her irises.

Theresagrassyknollonahill

A knock comes from the door to the room. Both of them turn as three figures break their privacy. One sports a long white overcoat, with the name *Dr. Paulsen* written in curvy blue letters on top of her breast pocket. The two men who walk in with her are sporting uniforms which mirror the blue, but in a darker hue. The wire of a radio cuts across each of their chests, snaking up the side of their uniforms.

"May we come in?" Dr. Paulsen asks, clipboard in hand. Her face reminds Stephen of a college professor – spectacled, with a cheerily absent voice. Her wrinkled, dark skin has been saturated by thankfulness and woe. She looks almost like an older version of Oprah, which would be fitting due to the Baltimore connection. The two officers beside her are agents of the same emotions. One of them is an Asian man with a straight face and a hardened demeanor, the other olive skinned and shorter with greaser hair and a wide grin.

"I'm pleased to see you're awake, Mr. Christiansen. We've been waiting on you to stir so we can finally meet Baltimore's next superstar," Dr. Paulsen walks over to the right side of Stephen's bed. Stephen raises his hand autonomously to meet the doctor's waiting palm.

"I'm Beth Paulsen, one of the trauma surgeons here at Johns Hopkins. I performed your shoulder surgery this evening, as well as bandaging that noggin of yours to prevent the next great American novel from seeping out of your ears," She pats Stephen on his good shoulder.

"Thank you, Dr. Paulsen. You saved my life," Stephen replies; his throat is suddenly dry, the words chewy.

"No, don't thank me, thank these two gentlemen," Dr. Paulsen gestures to the officers standing by her side. "These are officers Vincent Acampora and Jeremy Cheung. They responded to the call you made."

Stephen nods to the men. The one he assumes to be Acampora,

with the olive skin, steps forward to shake his hand, followed by his compatriot.

"Thank you so much, gentlemen," Stephen says.

"No problem, sir, we were doing our jobs," The raven-haired Acampora replies.

"When you have a moment, they would like to talk to you a little bit more about the incident." Dr. Paulsen says.

"Did you catch the two guys?" Stephen scratches his back with his good arm.

"Yes, sir, they're currently in custody," Officer Acampora replies. "We saw the one in the leather jacket hit you as we arrived at the scene. We also found his gun in close proximity to your body. When we were walking up to you, well ..."

Acampora coughs.

"It didn't look good," Stephen finishes his sentence for him.

"Exactly. See, this is why you're the author and not me," Acampora's laugh reveals neat white teeth.

"No, no, you guys are the ones who do the real work," Stephen says, raising the incline of his backboard. "I write, you guys save lives."

"Jeremy here is a huge fan of your work, actually. He's acting all shy behind me," Acampora turns to his partner. The other officer nods quickly, stepping forward for his own handshake.

"Officer Jeremy Cheung. I'm a great fan of yours, Mr. Christiansen," His voice is as firm and steady as his grip.

"Fucking ... why?" Stephen asks, dazed.

The entire room shares a burst of laughter.

"I like the plots," Jeremy responds, returning to his stately posture.

"Jesus, man, you need to read more," Stephen shakes his head.

A couple inches in either direction.

"I will, as soon as your next novel comes out," Jeremy replies.

"Trust me, men," Stephen looks at the three of them. "I'm a much bigger fan of your work today than you are of mine."

"It's the least we could do, Mr. Christiansen," Officer Acampora nods again. "You disobeyed every piece of sound advice your momma, or your fiancée, ever told you, and you came out relatively unscathed. You got extremely lucky for doing the right thing," Acampora shares a quick glance with Phoebe, who has moved closer to Stephen. She clutches his forearm close to her chest.

"She's a real trip, you know," Acampora says, laughing. Phoebe's smile widens. Dr. Paulsen flips through charts on her clipboard like a fast-cut reel of film. "Especially for a girl from Pennsylvania."

"Hey," Phoebe says. "I told you that in confidence! People don't need to know I'm from the sticks."

The officers laugh. Stephen's head throbs.

"We'll give you two a little time, and then if you're feeling up to it later tonight, or even in the morning, they need an official statement regarding your version of the incident," Dr. Paulsen checks Stephen's bandage on his left shoulder as she talks. "Does that sound alright with you, Stephen?"

"Yes, of course," Stephen replies, scanning the officers in front of him. "Again, thank you guys so much for all you've done for me. I truly have no way to repay you."

"Keep doing what you do, Mr. Christiansen," Acampora adjusts his radio. "Your stories could save someone's life someday. Jeremy over here wants a signed copy of your latest if you've got a chance."

Officer Jeremy flashes a large, happy face, and two thumbs up to Stephen.

"Absolutely. Anything you want—that goes for you too, Dr. Paulsen."

"What I want is for you to recover and to stop throwing yourself in the line of fire," Dr. Paulsen lets the papers fall to rest.

"That's our job," Acampora winks at Stephen as he and Jeremy turn to leave. "Take care Mr. Christiansen, we'll talk to you in the morning."

"You as well," Stephen replies.

"Now," Dr. Paulsen says as she reaches the door. "We'll send in the other visitor who's been waiting for you to rejoin the world of the living, if you're so inclined."

Neither Stephen or Phoebe object, and Phoebe nods.

"Sure."

Dr. Paulsen nods and leaves the room. Stephen can barely see her beckoning to someone in the hallway.

The door frame is filled by a man in a simple black jacket. He's wearing a reserved white dress shirt, his hands in the pockets of his fading jeans, which arch down over top of the work boots guarding his shins. His glasses aren't unlike Paulsen's, but are of a cheaper frame, holding a different kind of knowledge. His hair is tightly packed underneath a modest cap.

"Hello, Mr. Christiansen," the man says as he enters the room. "My name is Isaac Sellers. You saved my life today."

[5]

Around the restaurant, couples sit across small tables nestled next to the walls. Sports fans line the bar, entertained as much by the attractive brunette waitress as the games flashing on the televisions. Stephen sits with his back against the plastic of the booth, his feet resting on the bottom legs of the table. His hand touches the cup of coffee lightly as his left shoulder simmers.

"So," Stephen adjusts his dress shirt. "You're claiming I saved your life?"

Isaac, in the middle of taking a swig of his own coffee, nods. He's wearing the same jacket he wore the night he met Stephen in the hospital, and he bears a wedding band on his hand.

"You did," Isaac says. He sets his cup down gently.

Finally brave enough to sample his drink, Stephen shrugs as if he's brushing off needless praise. The heat is strong, flowing into the pit of his stomach. A silence hangs in the air like the punt in the football game blaring on the televisions. The bar men cheer at the action.

"How?" Stephen asks, scratching his neck with his good hand.

Dodging Stephen, Isaac peers into his empty cup.

"You did. You know you did."

"From what I remember," Stephen picks up a packet of sugar, ripping the seal and pouring it quickly. "It was you who knocked the gun out of that guy's hand after he already shot me once."

"Did I?" Isaac asks. "I suppose I did. I don't see how that saved your life, though."

Halting the coffee halfway through its arc to his mouth, Stephen laughs.

"Really?" Stephen asks.

Pinching an empty creamer container between his fingers, Isaac shakes his head.

"How do you suppose you *didn't* have a part in saving my life?" Stephen continues.

"Because," Isaac says, tossing the empty creamer aside. "If you hadn't stopped those two from robbing me, I would've died."

Furrowing his brow, Stephen leans back, and his bandaged shoulder winces in protest.

"Why do you assume you die if I don't show up?"

All shiftiness is gone as Isaac meets Stephen's gaze.

"Because I hadn't called the cops. They would've showed up too late. Nobody interferes for people like me. If it'd been you on the street, and anything seemed to be happening to you, the cops would've been called by everyone in a three block radius with help from any neighbor with a firearm," Isaac says.

"I don't think people would've intervened for me, either. It seemed stupidly barren, nobody was out."

"How is it possible for nobody to be out, or close by, on a crowded street in the late afternoon?" Isaac asks. "You think people hear there's violence outside and stay in their homes? I don't think so. Why did you have to be the one to call the police?"

"Because I walked right into it. I saw what was happening to you and decided to do something," Stephen smiles. "The officer called me stupid later in the day."

"Oh, you are stupid," Isaac laughs. "You're real stupid, walking up on a situation like that and trying to play hero."

"Well, it seemed to pay off."

"You got lucky."

"I thought you said I saved you?"

"You did."

"So then how was that stupid if it saved you?"

"It just was," Isaac says, clearing his throat. "People like me aren't supposed to get saved, Mr. Christiansen. You messed up the natural order. I was supposed to get shot that day."

"Why would you have been shot?"

"You think I'm going to let them take a paycheck's worth of medicine?" Isaac leans back in his chair. The wood creaks. "I was going to either convince them to let me go, or I was going to go Street Fighter on them and smash that gauged guy's head against the wall while his partner lit me up."

The screen flashes replays of a touchdown, a universe away.

"What kind of medication was it, if I can ask?"

"It was for me. It's pretty expensive nowadays."

"Didn't your insurance cover it?" Stephen asks.

Only a puff of humorless air serves as Isaac's response.

The interrupting absence of words swallows the space between them. A waitress arrives with their entrees. Stephen's ordered a Reuben burger, while Isaac's ordered a cheeseburger. Isaac pushes the fries to the side; they curl in their grease dejectedly. He plops a drop of ketchup onto the center of the burger. Placing the top half of the bun overtop the ketchup, he spreads it around. Stephen attempts not to choke on the onions he's trying to chew.

"What?" Isaac asks, pausing the motion of the bun.

"Nothing," Stephen says, his mouth full.

"You're an odd man, Mr. Christiansen. You've never seen someone use ketchup before?"

"Not like that," The mushrooms from the burger stick to Stephen's molars.

Isaac bites into the burger hesitantly.

"I'm a huge fan of your work, you know," Isaac says.

"I'll ask you what I asked the officers," Stephen blots mushroom juice from his chin. "Why?"

"You know why," Isaac replies, setting his burger on the table. Stephen's is already half eaten.

"I don't know, I guess as a writer I think all my stuff is shit no matter what anybody says."

"I know the feeling. I'm a writer too," Isaac replies, flicking one of the flaccid fries. "These things are like tiny mice tails stuck in a fryer."

"You should put some ketchup on them, that'd help. Rub it all over the top again."

This time, Isaac's laughter isn't forced.

"Phoebe told me you're married?" Stephen wipes his fingers with a napkin.

"Yep, that'd be correct. I'm married. I'd love for you to meet my wife sometime."

"I should be married, too."

"You aren't married?"

"Nope," Stephen's appetite dissipates.

"No offense, but the two of you struck me as a married couple," Isaac says.

Raising his hand like a comedian appealing to an audience, Stephen says, "Please tell my dear fiancée that when we finally manage to meet each other's better halves."

"Did she inspire Clarissa in *Trooper's Daughter*?"

The question draws a wary stare from the author.

"What do you mean?"

"Small town chick, hitches herself away from her oppressive family with some hotshot aspiring grad whilst she's at college, the two form a close bond only breakable by, and I quote, 'the unforgiving fists of time,' if I recall correctly."

Padding his shirt with another napkin, Stephen relents. "Ok, so you are a fan."

"I swear man, you're the next John Green," Isaac takes another bite, careful not to touch the other half he's cut.

"No way, I'm nowhere close to being anywhere near his level."

"No, you are. One day you'll pop up on the Oprah Winfrey show, and I'll turn to my wife and be able to say, 'Look honey, I had lunch with that guy! He saved my life that one time.'"

The words nearly make Stephen choke on his water.

"Yeah, alright, I'll see it for myself when the day comes."

"Oh, you'll be extremely successful," Isaac finishes half of the burger, and then sets the remaining half down next to the fries. The waitress—the same pretty brunette who'd been gawked at earlier—walks to them and asks if they need anything else. Isaac quietly asks for a box for the remaining food.

"You said you're a writer as well?" Stephen asks as the waitress clears the table.

"Indeed I am," Isaac says, folding his hands.

"Amazing. I knew there was a reason I stepped in to help you!"

"I think there's a reason for a lot of things that happen in our lives. I guess this was God's way of realizing one of my dreams, albeit by less than ideal circumstances. I didn't mean it when I said I'd die to meet you, you know. No offense to you."

"None taken. Well, if you ever want me to look over something of yours, feel free to let me know. My work and home emails are pretty straightforward," Stephen takes out a pen, and scribbles on the nearest clean napkin. He passes the item to Isaac.

"Seriously?" Isaac's expression shifts as he looks up from the folded white square. Suddenly he's a five year old kid at a Christmas village.

"Absolutely. I always love talking to people about their work. It's why I became an editor, after all," Stephen shoulders his jacket as the waitress returns with the bill.

"Thank you so much. Wow," Isaac says, chuckling. He tucks the napkin into his breast pocket and rises to shake Stephen's hand.

"Be in touch soon, my friend," Stephen takes out his wallet and points it at Isaac, almost accusingly. "And don't get mugged in the meantime. I've only got one good shoulder left."

The two walk towards the exit; the space between them resonates in a comfortable silence, the guttural laughter of the bar chasing them into the life of the night.

[6]

"Hey baby," Phoebe says.

"Hey, I've been waiting for you to call."

"I know. How was work?" she asks.

"Fine. Not really too busy for a Friday night, surprisingly."

"That's good to hear. Did your boss stop giving you shit?"

"Yeah. It only took around half a year for him to stop riding me."

"Poor you. You've got so many problems."

"You know it. Are you ready for next weekend?"

"Oh yeah, I'm all packed. I'm excited to get the hell out of this city for a couple days. We're still planning on leaving next Friday, right?"

"Yeah, I made the reservations already. We'll leave from Baltimore at around 5, if that's alright with you? We should be able to make it to Pennsylvania by eight, if traffic's not bad. I don't know exactly how many people are going to be traveling, but if history serves me right we'll have an easy drive."

"We'll stay at the Hilton for how long?" Phoebe asks.

"Two nights. I shall have you back home and in your scrubs ready to go for work Monday morning."

"Oh, *you'll* have me in my scrubs? You want to dress me now?"

"I think I'd much rather strip you completely naked, but if you insist."

"Look at you, Mr. Preparation! You've got everything figured out, don't you?"

"You know it. How's the job been? Seen anything disgusting recently?" he asks.

"Nope, it's been pretty uneventful. Everyone at work offered condolences, saying it was insane that my fiancé found his way on the news. Only the guy who I'm supposed to marry would actually pull a superhero act and fling himself in front of bullets for a person on the street. Why not call the cops and walk away?" Phoebe's disgust is palpable.

"Beats me. How is he doing, anyway?"

"He's recovered pretty quickly. The bullet exited his shoulder clean through the muscle and the tissues, missed the arteries, managed to come out the other side without taking a whole lot of important stuff with it. I think he'll recover fully in a couple weeks."

"That's good to hear. Can't have him getting too far off schedule, you know. He needs to stay focused."

"I hope for our sake he continues to stay focused. He's been on a major trip since the shooting. He's shoved himself away in our room banging words out until the wee hours of the morning."

"I'd like to bang you until the wee hours of the morning," Adam says.

"Stop it, he might hear us!"

"Oh shit, he's home right now?"

"No, I'm kidding. He's out having dinner with the guy who got him shot."

"Really?"

"Yeah, really. I talked to him in the ... what the hell are those things called? The waiting area? Receptionist desk? I work in a hospital, I swear."

"Yeah, the waiting area."

"Me, the two cops, and the guy who was getting robbed—the doctor was there too for a minute, but she couldn't give two shits—we talked for a little while about how courageous it was for Stephen to intervene. Apparently the dude is pretty disenfranchised financially."

"God, you sound so smart. Using words like *disenfranchised*."

"Well, I am engaged to a writer," Phoebe says.

"How much longer? I need to know when to buy the breakup novel."

"Asshole. I don't know, I mean, I'm pretty content at the moment with the way things are. He hasn't asked me to marry him for a while. He seems nonplussed."

"You're not happy, though."

"I am right now. I'm talking to you."

"Aw, how sweet. Do I get an invite to your guys' wedding?"

"That might not be a good idea, especially since there never will be any wedding."

"We should invite him to ours."

"Now that would be a plot twist."

"I'll twist your plots."

"Shut up, you pervert. You have to wait your turn until the weekend."

"My turn? Are you two planning on doing anything in the meantime?"

"No. What do you think? That hasn't happened for a while."

"So what, last week?"

"Yeah. We almost did it before he went to work one morning, but he's been having these stupid dreams every night which are keeping him awake."

"About what? Is this some insane writer's block shit?"

"They're weird. It's like, he says he's standing in a grassy field, and this hill keeps rising out of the ground ... why are you laughing?"

"That's some repressed sexual tension if I ever heard it."

"Jesus Christ, Adam! Are you driving? Can you still pay attention to the road with one hand on your dick?"

"What can I say, I can't help myself."

"You'd think after dealing with my shit for four years, you'd probably have cooled off by now."

"Uh, you made me wait for two of those four while you screwed around with Stevie to actually finally give me a shot. I'm damaged. I have issues."

"Oh, we both have issues."

"I know. One of them is abbreviated S.C."

"Stop it. He's not bad. It's me, not him."

"Fame does that to you. It clouds your mind and smudges what's really important in life."

"That was profound for a sexually-driven 'cog in the wheel of society' that spends his days working for the man."

"Says the nurse who loves him."

"I do love you," Phoebe says.

"I know," Adam replies.

"Well, he's going to be home soon. I'm gonna kill him if he brings that random guy with him. You know what he told me when we were talking?"

"What who told you?"

"The guy? The guy Stephen got shot over?"

"What?"

"He's married. And he's on *clozapine*, of all things. The dude's a schizoid, and *he's* the one who's actually married, not me and my *wonderful* fiancé!"

"You don't really want to be married."

"I used to."

"That's before you finally found me."

"Right."

"Ok, not before you found me, but before you actually gave me a chance."

"I'm glad I did."

"I'm glad you did, too. Hopefully, one day we'll stop screwing around like this."

"One day it'll happen."

"Sure, like your wedding to Stevie."

"Exactly. Alright, I'll let you get back to downshifting. Don't think about me too much, don't want to spoil yourself for the weekend."

"I got cruise control for a reason. Love you, Phoebe."

"Love you too. Bye."

"Bye."

Returning to its post on the wall, the receiver triggers a soft click which echoes through the empty apartment.

[7]

The Following Sunday Night

The handle makes a small thud against the wall as Phoebe removes her keys from the lock. Scuffing her feet on the carpet in the foyer, she hears the typing in the den seize. She can see that the light in the kitchen is turned on. The quadrangle of the apartment feels condensed. The crown of Stephen's head rests against the soft fabric of the couch, and his laptop hums in the shadow of the muted television. A dirty bowl sits like a rook on the armrest.

"Welcome home!" Stephen says, turning around to her.

Her cheeks are flushed red, most likely from the cold.

"Hey!" Phoebe says, removing her shoes. She wiggles slightly to adjust her wrinkled lingerie.

"How was the drive back?" Stephen closes his computer and sets it aside on the coffee table.

"It was fine, nothing too bad. Sunday nights are never that busy."

On her way towards the bedroom, she stops to kiss him, the small bristles of his face tickling her chin.

"Damn, that's some nice gum," Stephen says, smiling a bit as she walks away. "Peppermint?"

"Spearmint," Phoebe enters the bedroom and deposits her purse on top of the ruffled sheets. Walking into the adjunct bathroom, she looks in the mirror and pulls her hair up with a hand so she can see her neck. She then raises her shirt to observe her midriff, a delicate tattoo of a rose tracing her stomach. She sighs, pulls down on her bra, and flattens her shirt. Content, she reaches into her pocket and returns the engagement ring to her left hand. Stephen hears her pad across the carpet into the living room, and puts his phone away. Both he and Facebook are getting older.

Walking around the couch, Phoebe hops into Stephen's waiting arms. The two laugh, and Phoebe sprawls her legs out on the cushions, her head in Stephen's lap. The light from the television and the room dances on the blue of her eyes like sparks pirouetting across a frozen lake.

"Hello there," Stephen says.

"Hi. Nice to meet you. I'm Phoebe Walker," she says back.

"Hey, Phoebe. Fancy seeing you here. I've missed you since the last time we talked."

"I missed you too. My mom's house is great and all, but it gets pretty lonely."

"How's your mom doing?"

"She's doing well, from what I can tell. It was nice to be able to spend some quality time with her away from all this noise. I'm always surprised how quiet the country is."

"How's Grace?"

"She's doing great, actually. She and Eddie bought a new house somewhere in the rural, rollin' hills of Pennsylvania, but it's farther up in the county, so that makes it different than the middle of nowhere."

"That's some sound logic," Stephen chuckles.

"Yup. That's how she's always rolled. You know how it goes; I'm the sister, and I'm younger, so my opinion is worth about as much as a French translator at a bullfight in Spain."

"That's a good one."

"You should use it in your next book," She begins poking at one of the buttons on Stephen's shirt. "How is that going, by the way?"

"Well," Stephen says, playing with a few strands of her hair, his other hand resting on top of her stomach. "I'm sort of mind-numbed at the moment, actually. I've written a couple thousand words and instantly deleted them."

"Really? That's odd. You typically find it pretty easy to write all your projects at once, don't you?"

"Yeah. I guess it's probably the backlog from work catching up with me."

"Are you behind?"

"Yeah. Shultz is getting angry. I've been shaky on focusing during the day; it must be the lack of sleep."

"Don't tell me you're still dreaming about me," Phoebe says.

"No, I don't even remember them half the time. They leave me lying awake every couple of hours."

"Do you think you need therapy?"

He squeezes her hand. "I think I've got all I need right here."

They stare at each other for a moment. Stephen starts to ask a question, but then changes his mind.

"What?" Phoebe asks.

"Nothing."

"Come on, tell me. What?"

Words, long repeated and often suppressed, leak out of Stephen's mouth like carbon monoxide.

"I think we should get married," Stephen says plainly.

Even though the television's muted, it now steals Phoebe's attention instead of her fiancé's sound.

"Steve, we've had this conversation at least once every three months. I've wanted to get married for a while—since you proposed—but we can't right now."

"It's been seven years. How many couples wait seven years to get married?"

"I know a few. It took my parents a while."

"Seven years?"

"No. Two," Phoebe sighs.

"Two was too quick, I agree."

"And then we tried to start planning around three, and then you got signed," Phoebe says absently, as if recalling a history class.

"Four was blocked by the release and the tour," Stephen segues. "And then five by your new shift at Sinai."

"Then year six was blocked by *Calls*, plus the fact I was working *double* shifts at Sinai and couldn't keep my head on straight," Phoebe looks back to him with a matter-of-fact air.

"Now we're on eight, and it seems like things are happening," Stephen says.

"Like what?"

"Well, *Calls* is trending upward, I'm finally past all the demons and the doubt, and we've stayed together through all the ups and downs and you keep coming back to me for some stupid reason."

Pressing her cheek against Stephen's knee, Phoebe's dimples recede.

"I don't know, Steve. Aren't things fine the way they are now?"

"Didn't you say you've wanted to get married this entire time?"

"Yeah, but ..."

"But what? You like the name 'Phoebe Walker' better than 'Phoebe Christiansen'?"

"It's complicated to change all that stuff."

Laughing, Stephen places his hand gently on the side of her face, turning her back to him.

"Listen." Stephen whispers. With that word, she can see the face of the 21 year old college Senior who popped the question in a field of December lights.

"When I met you, I had no idea who I was. I didn't know who I wanted to be; I only had some passing ideas of dreams long forgotten and people who shaped my life. My mom's death still hung over my head, my dad's hopes a chalk outline on a forgotten street back in a small town where nobody aspires to be anything. But then I met this girl who was from a similarly small Pennsylvania town with the same kind of disposition, set against the world like a traveler caught in history. She was the most beautiful person I'd ever seen, with her spirit both as pretty as an angel and as boundless as freedom. I dated this girl for two years, and I learned what it was like to love for the first time. I learned how to let the past be the past, how to not fear being myself. When I asked this girl to marry me under a sky of stars at Christmastime, I knew I'd found the person who made me whole. I saw her complete her degree, stand with me through mounds of rejection letters, and buy this quaint little apartment on the West side of Baltimore so she could pursue her passion while I found my path. I've dedicated books to her, written testaments to her through the work which defines my life, but I want to shout, and scream, and finally show the world how much she means to me. There doesn't have to be a bunch of lights or fancy decorations, because no reception hall or banquet can hold the wealth of who you are. I love you, Phoebe Walker. No matter what we go through or the downward spirals we face, I will always love you, and I want to marry you."

The slender tears form at the corners of Phoebe's eyelids, and the ensuing kiss feels empty. After a few seconds, she pulls away and lies her head back down in his lap, blinking until the salty drops trace her cheekbones.

She shakes her head. Stephen frowns at her.

"I'm not ready, Stephen."

Almost as if he's zooming out a microscope, Stephen reexamines her, dissecting her features with care.

"I'm not ready," she says again. "Next year looks a lot better. I want to get out of this town. I want us to build a house together—a real house, not an apartment, where we can raise a family. I want you to fly, and spread your wings, and become the amazing author I know you are, but I also know I'm not ready yet."

"Where do we need to move to?" Stephen asks, his voice rising. "Where do we have to go so you can be happy?"

"I can be happy right here. I love the way we are, but I don't see how marriage changes anything. Marriage implies we need something to be different."

Lowering his voice, Stephen leans his head back, his hands covering his face.

"Someday, baby. It'll happen," Phoebe says. She rises from his lap, moving to the cushion next to him, and puts her arm around his neck. She pecks him on the cheek, and he turns his attention to the television.

"You promise? One of these days we're actually going to go through with this?" He looks directly at her; her eyes have returned to their regular, solid blue instead of watercolor.

"I promise. I love you with all my heart and soul."

With that, her head finds the crook of his shoulder as Stephen um-mutes the television. Fifteen minutes later, she's sleeping softly, her chest fluttering with each breath. Stephen can only look down and wonder.

[8]

There's a grassy knoll nestled onto the side of a hill, and she's no longer there.

He's alone, standing amidst the tilting stalks of wheat. Shadows descend around him from the passing clouds. Away from the knoll, there's a fork in the road, with a path branching in both directions. Stephen opens and closes his eyelids, and the knowing insensibility which powers all dreams brings him to the crossroads. The knoll behind him breaks the cool wind.

He takes a look around him, and she's there down the path on the right! She's transparent, like a ghost popped out of a broken tombstone; a sunbeam caught in the remnants of a raincloud. She's at least fifty yards down the road, which extends into the universe beyond the horizon of his sight. He uses her as a reference point, and the distance seems small, but infinite.

He whets his lips, and prepares a shout. It catches in his windpipe, forcing him to cough. He tries again, yet the sound is trapped. His breathing slows, and he can no longer seem to siphon the sweet air into his lungs. Both of his hands flash to his throat, and the words expand, filling his airway like a demented balloon. As he struggles, she keeps on drifting backwards down the right path, and he reaches out a hand as his senses fail.

His world goes black, and

"Stephen?"

Stephen snaps upright; his face is covered by small black dots. The piece of paper falls off his skin and flutters safely to the desk. He coughs, and his breathing steadies. The hair upon his head is scraggly, and his chin is unshaven. The sleeves on his shirt are rolled up, his jacket draped lazily over the left arm of his chair. The pen which had been in his hands rolls off the side of the desk with a small thud.

With an eyebrow raised, Shultz enters from the hallway.

"Dude, what the hell?"

Stifling a yawn, Stephen peels away the curtain of sleep.

"Sorry, Charlie. I was taking five."

"More like fifteen. You've got ink all over your face."

On his desk, next to the edits-in-progress, the clock says 2:32.

"Weird, I could've sworn I was only out for around five minutes," Stephen groggily blinks at the intrusive sunlight from the window.

"I've checked on you three times today, and each time it looks like you're ready to use your desk as a sleep number mattress like its *siesta* time in kindergarten. Is something up?"

"Nah, man," Stephen stretches. The normal picture of he and Phoebe, with the two of them smiling in front of Camden Yards, has been joined by an older image of the two silhouetted by a massive Christmas tree. Youth twinkles in their silhouettes.

"Come on, don't bullshit me. This is the second time you've been catching up on sleep on company time this week, and it's only Thursday."

"Yeah, but Tuesday and Wednesday were alright, right?"

"Well, actually, no, they could've been better. I managed to catch an error you missed."

"What?" Stephen subdues another yawn. He picks his pen up off the floor.

"In the fourth manuscript revision of *Baker's Thirteen*, you managed to actually omit an entire page of the draft which you were copyediting. I'm unsure whether you accidentally deleted it, or if it's included in the rash of items stuck to your face, but come on. We can't be stepping out of line now; you're usually spotless."

"Who comes up with a name like *Baker's Thirteen*, anyway?" Stephen looks into the empty coffee mug—proudly displaying the title *best boyfriend ever!*—and turns it over, letting the residue from his drink spill out onto the top of his desk like small, brown raindrops.

"What are you doing? How many cups of that shit did you drink this morning?" Shultz walks across the room and stands in front of Stephen's desk: a menagerie of loose papers, pens, a stapler, the pictures, and now the coffee drops. His laptop sits proudly amongst the clutter.

"I don't know, man. I haven't been sleeping that much."

"Why is that? Is Phoebe up your ass again?"

"What? Don't say that," Stephen snaps as he places the mug back down.

"I'll take that as a yes," Shultz pulls a spare napkin from the inside of his immaculate suit and blots the table.

"Cut it, Charlie. She hasn't been doing anything," Stephen sighs and rests his chin on his hands. "I'm the problem, not her."

"Oh for the love of Christ, did you ask her to marry you again?"

"Yup."

"And she said no?"

"She said she's still not ready. She said she wants to be in the position to raise a family first, and our apartment isn't cutting it."

"My apologies to your unborn children, but you're doing the best you can. I wish we were larger—we'd be able to pay you more, but your book sales are about to spike and that might give you the influx you need. But ... who cares? You're still on the rise, and in a position most people hardly dream about for fear of disappointment. Doesn't she understand that?"

"Yes, she understands that. She understands that more than anybody, except for you," Stephen examines the two pictures on the right side of his desk.

"Which picture is that? Is that from that place back near her hometown, the ... farmer's whorehouse or whatever?" Shultz asks, pointing to the frame on the right.

"Peddler's Village, yeah."

"Close enough."

"Yeah, that's from the year I proposed to her. We were juniors. So much prosperity and hope in the gazes of those who are innocent to what the future holds."

"Go back to sleep, Shakespeare."

"It's true. If you'd have told me back then I'd be lucky enough to call that girl in my arms my fiancée, to have someone to truly call my own, who loved me for who I was—I would've never believed you."

"The kid in that picture probably would've expected you two to be married by now," Shultz says, his tone sharp.

"No," Stephen says, sitting up straight and adjusting his collar. He buttons his shirt quickly. "Lots of people wait. I'm waiting until she's ready, and she's right. We're in no position to have a family at the moment."

"Honestly though, there's not a whole lot that's different when you're married, it just makes it official – stylistically, that is," Shultz shrugs. "The ring is nice and all, but there's something about the title of husband and wife which does add a new dimension, plus all the legalities. Maybe she doesn't want to give up the name Walker?"

"That doesn't make sense. I think I'm pressuring her too much, and it's driving her away from the idea."

"Fuck me sideways," Shultz says, rubbing his temples. "You ask her what, once every six months what the plans are?"

"About."

"That's not pressure, that's common sense."

"She needs a bit more time."

"What, another seven years?"

"Charlie."

"What, Steve?" Shultz's humor evaporates, and he steps around to the front of Stephen's desk again. "I think this is a raft of shit. I love Phoebe to death, but this makes absolutely no sense, and it's driving you insane, which is driving my profit margin down with each moment you're asleep on the clock."

"I'm sorry. I keep having this stupid recurring dream which wakes me up during the night."

"It's the closeted emotions you're blinded by seeping into your skull and harassing your brain with how far your head is up your own ass."

Massaging his temples, Stephen wakes his computer by swiping a finger across the track pad. His inbox blinks to life on the screen, and his eyes sting as they focus on the change in brightness. He'd cleared the new messages prior to falling asleep.

"Well, do me a favor and don't make me fire you, alright? You're integral to this company's success, but I can't have my editors passing out on the job, no matter how many times they saved me from a drunken stupor ten years ago, champ. Put her out of your mind, you're not doing anything wrong," Shultz says.

"Easier said than done," Stephen says, wiping off a small bit of coffee which Shultz's tissue hadn't grabbed.

"It'll be a lot easier for all of us if you find a way to stay awake. Snort some drugs or something, that's what all writers do, isn't it?"

The resulting smile from Stephen is bogged down by the weight of the bags on his face. "Something like that."

Shaking his head, Shultz returns to the bowels of the Bessemer offices, most likely to harass one of the other editors. A ding springs from the laptop's speakers. Stephen clicks the refresh button, and a new email sits at the top of his inbox.

"Manuscript?" Stephen mutters as he opens the message. "Our submission window closed two weeks ago."

Dear Mr. Christiansen,

Thank you so much for dinner last week, I deeply enjoyed myself! You are a humble legend. First you save my life and then you treat me to a meal? I am truly blessed. I was wondering if you'd be interested at all in meeting up once again, this time to discuss the document which I have attached to this email. You mentioned potentially being interested in reviewing work of mine, so I rummaged together a few writings in order to give you a general idea of what my writing is like. Any feedback you'd be willing to give would be *INVALUABLE* to me, and if you are too busy to spare any time I completely understand.

One day, you're going to be on television, and like I said, I'm going to turn to my wife and say, "That man saved my life!" :)

I look forward to hearing from you soon,

Isaac Sellers

"Dammit, Isaac," Stephen mutters, sitting up straight in his chair. Ignoring the papers strewn across his desk, Stephen opens the document and begins to read, the waning sunlight of the afternoon sky peeking through the office window.

PART II

[9]

The glowing red bird observes them from his perch on the wall. Stephen half expects it to detach and land on his head in a burst of crimson feathers. Odd pieces of Americana serve as the décor like photos in a scrapbook.

"So, what exactly is this?" Stephen asks, holding up the stapled pages in his hands. Isaac places his unfolded napkin in his lap.

"It's me," His words are laced with parental magic.

"I'm aware of that. I read through most of it last night," The margins are dotted with the red blood of Stephen's pen.

"Really? You didn't have to do that," Isaac laughs. "Lord, if someone would've told me Stephen Christiansen would be sitting across from me commenting on my stupid stories, I never would've believed them."

Biting his tongue, Stephen truly believes that *he needs to stop saying that kind of shit.*

"So, this is somewhat of a narrative?" Stephen asks.

"Sort of," Isaac shifts around in the booth. "I'd say it's mostly autobiographical, but in a way that's a synthesis of fiction and memoir."

"A *Roman à clef* of sorts?" Stephen asks. Isaac raises his eyebrows.

"Is that what you call it?"

"Nevermind," Stephen says, returning to the papers.

"Some of us haven't taken all those fancy literature courses," Isaac winks at him.

"Good on you," Stephen replies.

"I've had a different type of … education, besides my schooling for graphic design," Isaac says, emphasizing the *education*.

"I gathered something along those lines. Some of the experiences in here are less than appealing, to say the least," Stephen offers. *Actually, they're extraordinarily shitty.*

"That's my life. Less than appealing fits the bill," Isaac's luminosity fades.

"That's why we're writers," Stephen reams through the pages carefully.

"It's not like we have a choice," Isaac agrees. "It filters the malevolence out of me, a siphon to a wound; it takes all the pain I could press onto others and instead puts it on the printed page."

"That's pretty poetic," Stephen says.

"Wouldn't you know it? I used to be a preacher."

"A what?" Stephen stops tracing the pages.

"A preacher."

"Like, in a church?"

"Yup. Had my own 500 person congregation comprised of folks from Baltimore."

"That's incredible. Do you still preach?"

"Not anymore," Isaac says. Stephen waits, but he doesn't elaborate. They're interrupted, and they both lean back as the waiter, a young, chipper man with diamond studded ears, delivers their drinks. The glasses hit the table with a soft clatter, and they place their orders.

"Why don't you preach anymore?" Stephen asks, taking a sip of his iced tea.

Pushing the straw down with a finger, Isaac drinks from the cup, his lips smoothly touching the glass.

"It's hard to preach when you have questions, Stephen."

Snickering, Stephen's expression is that of a kid who got called out for texting during math class. Isaac puts his drink down.

"What?"

"I'm sorry," Stephen's laughter now draws tears, and he places the manuscript to the side.

Isaac's face resurfaces from the pensive dive of his past, and instead relaxes as Stephen regains his composure.

"What? Do you find the fact I don't preach anymore amusing, Mr. Christiansen?"

"Lord Jesus, no," Stephen clears his throat, his breath coming in bursts. "What did you do to that straw? Didn't you drink from the glass?"

"Oh," Isaac picks up his drink again, and demonstrates how he bends the top of the plastic.

"Why do you do that?" Stephen asks, his fingers fumbling as he tries to imitate the action.

"Because, you can never look cool when drinking from a straw," Isaac explains, taking another swig.

"I suppose you're right," Stephen picks up the glass, collapsing the black plastic with his index finger, and drinks.

The glass falls out of Stephen's hand and crashes onto the table. Tea shoots out with a collection of ice as it spills onto his jeans. Stephen jerks up from the table and Isaac jumps; the laughter which escaped Stephen has found a new home in Isaac's guffaws. Stephen looks helplessly from the lopsided glass, to Isaac, to his lap, back to Isaac, and finally shakes his fingers, causing small droplets of liquid to sprinkle the tabletop.

"Well," Stephen says. "Apparently I can't look cool either way."

Grabbing napkins from the holder, Isaac tosses them on top of the spill. They float like islands.

"God, you're so white," Isaac mutters. Stephen's glare has a hint of humor. Their waiter returns with more napkins.

"Would you like another tea, sir?" The waiter asks as he turns the glass upright.

"No thank you, I think I've got enough fluid at the moment,"

Stephen responds monotonously.

"Gee Mr. Christiansen, you sound pretty dry for being soaked," Isaac drums the table with a *ba – dum - tish*. His manuscript dodged the eruption successfully.

Soon, the table is dried and a tall, sweating glass of water is returned to Stephen's hands. Daintily, he leans down and drinks from the straw.

Shifting, Stephen winces at the coldness of his seat.

"So, I think we were talking about you no longer preaching?"

"Right," Isaac says, stirring the ice in his water. "I found it hard to preach once I couldn't convince myself of the words I spoke. I stopped believing in destiny as I got older."

"I see." Stephen says. "I wouldn't call myself a man of faith by my church attendance, but I do believe in Him."

"Going to church doesn't make you a believer. I was there for a long time and I had just as many doubts as you. I've read the Bible, I've based the wholeness of who I am as a part of His work, and I've spoken to Him many times."

"Has He ever gotten back to you?"

The stirring stops, and Isaac shakes his head.

"It's not He who speaks to me."

In an instant, Stephen's mouth is as dry as the table at which he sits. "Then who speaks to you?"

Isaac's stare is piercing.

"I'm never quite sure. Sometimes it's my sister, calling to me as if she's still a teenager, before her life fell apart. Other times I think its Satan. Well, one time he claimed to be Satan, I can't know for sure. He sure as hell didn't ask to trade me a golden fiddle for my soul."

The ice cubes bob in Stephen's drink.

"What do the voices say to you?" Stephen asks.

"To kill myself. Or worse, to kill Olivia."

"Your wife?" Stephen asks.

"Yup," Isaac says. Stephen notices the grit tracing Isaac's features, a hardened shell built up over years.

"They tell me all sorts of things, but that's their favorite message. They tell me to kill myself, or that I've failed Olivia, or that I should never even have been born. When my mother was pregnant with me, my Daddy held a gun to her stomach when they were getting out of a taxi cab," Isaac takes a drink from his cup.

"Jesus Christ." Stephen whispers.

Swallowing quickly, Isaac shakes his head.

"It's not Jesus. I've asked Jesus to make them stop, but they seem to amplify when I'm around people. They certainly didn't stop when I was in the hospital last year, or when the straight jacket enclosed me in a constricting embrace. He didn't put shoes upon my feet when I walked through the cold without a destination, and he didn't send me a paycheck when I begged."

"What do you mean when you walked through the cold?"

"I've walked through snow wearing a hoodie, jeans, and flip flips."

"Why?"

"I didn't have any other shoes."

"Were you ...?"

"Homeless, yes."

"For how long?"

"Four years."

"What?"

"I believe you asked me how health insurance would pay for my medication when we ate together the first time. I would be alright with having enough to pay for Olivia and mine's dinner all the nights of the week," A rogue wisp of humor traces Isaac's face. "If you want, you can contribute to the 'Feed Isaac Initiative', it's a popular new program opening right now in Baltimore."

"How are you talking to me right now?" Stephen asks. "Do you hear the voices?"

"Nope, I only hear yours and mine."

"The medication?"

"Yes."

"It stops the voices entirely?"

"Sort of. Mine remains, the one inside my head."

"What does it say to you?"

Draining the glass once again, Isaac regards Stephen the same way a parent tells their child about one of their elementary school classmates dying in a freak accident.

"To go home to God."

"It makes you want to go home to God?"

"That seems to be the most logical side effect, you know? The voices tell me to kill myself if I don't take the medication, and then the medication makes me a drudge. It de-motivates me, places me in this mindset that nothing good's ever coming and my best days have already passed. I ask myself why God would burden me, why I can't come home to Him and take away all this pain which lingers. You don't ever forget the feeling of wet snow falling between the open tops of your shoes, or having some bastard piss on you when you're trying to sleep because you've got nowhere to go."

"Someone pissed on you?" Stephen's voice rises.

"Yeah," Isaac chuckles. "At least he cared enough to notice me. Most people pass by with their vision locked to this level," Isaac places his hand on the crest of his brow. "They don't look down, and every time you're looking up all you see are the undersides of their chins."

Silence rises from the table like a mist.

"How are things in your life now?" Stephen finally manages.

"They're alright. Olivia and I have a small apartment on the northern side, we manage to keep up with the car payments and the rent. We've been married for almost two years now, but we've known each other since we were 19."

"That's awesome," Stephen's emotional barometer drops. *Married for two years.*

"It's us against the world, as she tells me," Isaac grins in a boyish way. "She's picked me up when I've been cast out by my own family, yelled back to silence the voices, captured my hatred and my disappointment; she absorbs all of it into the benevolent fibers of her soul."

All Stephen can do is nod.

"I guess that's why God's keeping me here, because of that kind of love," Isaac says.

Their conversation is interrupted by the arrival of their food. Isaac thanks the waiter, and Stephen grunts in recognition as he stares at the table. Stephen glances up, and notices Isaac cutting his burger in half.

"Why do you do that?"

"Hm?" Isaac responds, separating the bun.

"Why do you cut your burger like that before you even start eating? I saw you chewing it out that way the last time we met."

"Oh." Isaac says, putting the knife down. He picks up the ketchup bottle and sprays it underneath one half of the sandwich, rubbing it into the meat as he did before. "I save it for later, in case," Isaac places the ketchup back down. "You don't forget."

Staring at his own food, Stephen feels his face growing a balmy red. His stomach is the combination of a blender and an icebox. Isaac begins eating, and notices Stephen boring into the manuscript hiding near his left hand.

"Why aren't you eating, Steve?"

"I'm not hungry," Stephen replies.

"Oh. Was it the incident with the water?" Isaac stops eating, the burger halfway to his mouth. "I'm sorry I said anything."

"No, no, it wasn't that at all," Stephen quickly reaches into his wallet. "Here, I'll pay, I'm honestly not that hungry. You can have it, if you want."

Putting his food down, Isaac frowns. "Stephen, no, don't do that."

"No, I insist, I'm honestly not hungry man. Take it home. Here, I can even give you a little extra. It's $20, that's all I have," Stephen feels his eyes brimming with moisture. "I'm so sorry I said anything about the health insurance, I'm an idiot."

"Stephen?" Isaac chuckles.

Holding the money outstretched, Stephen sniffles.

"What? Come on man, what?"

"Stephen, you don't need to give me money. It has no value to me."

"What?"

"I've lived off the land via the wealth of love for my entire life, I'm extremely blessed. I'll take the material as it comes, my friend."

"Please, just take the $20. It's only a stupid burger, too, I mean—no, it's not a stupid burger, its food, I --"

Touching his outstretched hand, Isaac gets Stephen to stop talking.

"Stephen, you've already helped me enough, more so than I ever deserved, especially from someone like you."

Stephen sputters, the face on the bill crumpled.

"How? By getting shot?"

"Not even that," Isaac glimmers. "You listen."

[10]

The covers of the bed beneath Phoebe rustle as she adjusts herself in the room's descending twilight. A television on the mustardy wall chants indiscernible babble. Vaguely, the animations within the television's glass spin as the local Baltimore news anchors proclaim *October 10th, 2014* to be the date. Draping a pink, lacy shawl around her bare shoulders, she makes her way across the room past the other, unoccupied bed to the bathroom. Un-used *Do Not Disturb* signs clutter the handle of the door.

His shoulders at ease, Adam rests on the pillows pressing up against the headboard; the majority of his chest is now covered by the sheet. Two glasses of wine sit on the small table to his left. They'd left the windows open this time, figuring they were far enough off the ground; people have a manner of respect in this day and age. He picks up his glass, his head buzzing with the afterglow, his nose aloof with the scent of her perfume, and his ears holding onto every syllable of those three words:

I love you.

Returning from the bathroom, Phoebe slips back under the rustled sheets. Scooching over to him, she lays her head upon his shoulder, her spirit smiling as she feels his hand resting on her rose tattoo.

"So," Adam says. "Are you getting married yet?"

"No, I don't think so. You can never be too sure, it might happen one day."

"Right," Adam says, the bristles of his cropped chin bouncing as he chuckles. "One day you'll tell me we're done, and then you'll go live with him on some farmhouse in the country."

"Yeah, sure," Phoebe's tone is dismissive. She reaches across him and takes hold of her own wine, the bottle sitting on the table next to her engagement ring.

"Jesus, you guys are weird. I remember you guys talking about marriage back in 2012," Adam fumbles for the pack of cigarettes in the pocket of his jeans. Phoebe's blouse and pants lie tossed aside on the carpet.

"Was that before or after we started?" Phoebe asks playfully.

"I think 'this' happened after he asked you that time. I remember you being pretty upset."

"I'm always upset," She hooks onto his arm; a lit cigarette dangles from his lips.

"You're not upset when you're here," He says. He begins playing with a strand of her hair.

"You're right, I'm not. I wish I could be here all the time."

"I'm waiting to see which happens first: you get married, or you tell Stephen about us."

"He's never going to find out," Phoebe says. The reporter on the television, a black man in his middle 40's, is talking about the Orioles.

"Which? That we're a couple or that you're never getting married?" Adam asks, blowing a puff of smoke.

"Either," Phoebe grins, snuggling closer to him. She stretches a leg across his midsection, and his arm moves from her stomach to the small of her back, his head leaning into hers. "I want us to be able to stay like this."

"You should probably break up with him, then."

"I can't do that," Phoebe says.

"Why not?"

"I don't want to hurt him."

Starting at a chuckle, Adam's soon laughing so hard he's coughing, the cigarette bouncing in his hand. Phoebe looks at him quizzically.

"What?"

Calming himself, Adam shakes his head.

"You don't want to hurt him?" Adam repeats.

"I don't. I never wanted to hurt him."

"Well, I mean, if he finds out about this, I don't think he's going to be happy."

"I know," Phoebe says, resting on his chest. "That's why he's never going to find out."

"Then you're going to keep on being unhappy for him?" Adam asks, refilling his wine glass.

"I don't know. It seems to have worked so far."

"Yeah," Adam says, raising the glass to his lips. After swallowing, he adds, "But you did tell me about how you wish this could be *all the time* for both of us."

"I do. I wish there was a way he could realize we're not what he wants us to be. He's married to his craft, and I want something different."

"What does he want?" Adam asks, drinking again.

"He wants fame. He's wanted fame to prove his worth. He tried to find that in me first, and I couldn't give it to him. I'm a horrible girlfriend, fiancée—I'd be an awful wife."

"Don't say that," Adam pulls her closer. He notices her cheeks streaked with tears. "You'd be a wonderful wife. I'd like to make you mine someday."

Sniffling, like a girl who got told her parents were disappointed in her, Phoebe says, "I honestly wish I could've made it work for him, but he doesn't ... I don't know, he doesn't see me for me. He sees me as a character in one of his books. I love his books, I love his writing,

I loved him once, but I can't *be* who his mind creates."

"He's blind if he doesn't love you for what you are. If he's trying to make you like an image in his head, like an idea, he forgets the beauty that's real."

Phoebe shakes her head. "He forgot that a long time ago, somewhere over the past eight years. I can't throw myself into somebody else's black hole. We've been living in the same shit apartment, doing the same stupid routine, ever since he and Charlie started that company after we left college, and I'm so trapped. This is not who I promised to marry, and in the past few weeks he's been completely absorbed in his work."

"Since the shooting?" Adam asks. He finds his glass empty.

"Yeah. I think it triggered some sort of depressive relapse."

"I thought he got over that years ago."

"No," Phoebe says. "You never truly 'get over' something like that. It comes in cycles, and tragic events have a way of propelling it back to controlling your life. People don't understand mental illness. I held him when he cried in my lap after his Dad's passing, I promised to always stand by his side, but I could only give so much. I couldn't give it all," Her shoulders shake underneath Adam's arm.

"Hey," Adam says, lowering his voice. The cigarette bums in a portable ashtray on the table. "Stop it. You've been so good to him, he has no idea what he's throwing away."

"I was young and stupid. We both were," Phoebe's words are muddled by the rushing memories. "I truly thought we would conquer the world back then. I believe he still will, but I simply can't be with him. He traded 'us' for his success."

"Well, I for one am glad he threw you away, because I found somebody amazing. Do you remember when we met?"

"Yep. At Paul and Vicky's wedding, right?"

"I remember shaking Steve's hand and then being floored by this insanely beautiful fiancée of his," Adam wipes a tear from her cheek. "Right then, I knew we were supposed to be together. I remember we talked later that night, and Steve was busy bitching to Paul about the merits of publishing, and there are moments which are super-cut from some pocket of God which change your life, and we made one of those moments that night."

Smoothing the sheets with her hand, Phoebe comes to a conclusion. "I should tell him. I need to tell him. I don't want us to be dirty anymore, I don't want us to have to sneak around and hide, because this is how I want to be, how I want *us* to be."

"He remembers me?"

"Vaguely. He knows you know Paul, and he does have a good memory, especially since it was some wedding back in 2010."

"I remember him. From talking to him for those couple minutes, he seemed like a nice guy, but good lord is his ego as big as the Hindenburg," Adam picks the cigarette up from the ashtray.

"He honestly doesn't mean it," Phoebe says. "It's a reflex of when he was depressed. He had to find the small things to lift himself up to replace all the shit he dealt with in life, and he never stopped. It's made him extremely successful."

"But that's also made you extremely unhappy. Phoebe, I don't care about him. I don't wish ill on him in any way, but I hate the fact he treated you so badly."

"He never abused me."

"He didn't have to. Look at yourself. If you're not happy, then you need to find a way to change."

Her crying ceasing, she's silent for a moment. Her mind works quickly, and she opens her mouth to say the words, to put her treason into reality.

"I'm going to break up with him."

Adam sits up straight. "Really?"

"Yeah. You're completely right. I need to make myself happy, I need to stop lying, and I need to follow what's right for me. Will you take me in after it happens?" Adam sees her face turning crimson in the dim light of the hotel room.

Bearing the look of a skeptic, Adam says, "Gee, I don't know ... might be a bit of a stretch. I've only been waiting for you to say that for the past two years, I might have to say no."

"I'll do it sometime in the next month," She says with finality. She breathes in a deep mix of the corrupted air, and then exhales quickly.

"You don't think it's a little mean? Leaving him right after he's been shot?" Adam smiles. She's moved over to the other side of the bed, sitting on her haunches, her hands folded. He follows her and pulls her close.

"Please. He got so lucky, the bullet went straight through him— he hardly even needed the surgery. He's already fully recovered. He's been working non-stop and waking up at random hours. I'd feel sorry for him, but I can't. He's so rash, Adam. He stepped in front of those robbers for a stranger. How stupid can you be?"

"I'd take a bullet for you," Adam says.

"You're so cliché," Phoebe laughs, now unburdened. "I can tell you're not a writer."

"Oh, I'm cliché?" Their faces are inches apart. "You want to try calling me that again?"

Before she can, his lips are on hers. He picks her up and lies back on the bed, and she's on top of him, her shawl falling from her shoulders.

(11)

The laptop is the only light in the apartment. Dirty dishes from the past two days line the cushions next to Stephen, also covering the table in front of him. The rims of his eyes are overused and stretched, the arching magma of their bloodshot streaks coursing from the iris. The clothes he'd worn to work earlier in the day still cover his back; cans of iced tea litter the floor. As he moves a foot, they rattle like dyslexic jingle bells summoning Satan instead of Santa.

With his fingers in pole position on the keyboard, Stephen's having a staring contest with the screen. He's been attempting to win for the past six hours; she'd left to go out with her friends two days ago, to give him the solitude of these nights. He'd tried making love to her two days ago and hadn't been able to. He'd tried showing her how much he loved her by proposing, and she'd thrown it back in his face for the past eight years. While the events are both flaccid, only one stings him in the soul.

He shakes his head, and attempts to regain his train of thought. If he keeps handing in un-edited bits of scraps to Shultz, he'll get fired; it'll disenfranchise his finances, Phoebe will leave, and he'll have time to perfect his masterpiece, his ticket to fame, his *holy grail*. This generation's always needed a Sophocles, or perhaps a Baldwin or Orwell. He's got the next *Catch-22, 1984, Tuesdays with Morrie, Shock of the Fall* on the very tip of his tongue, the sinews of his fingertips.

theresagrassyknollonahilloneoneoneoneone

It's ready to be let out if he can only coax it. They'd told him at the hospital how they'd put the *great American novel* back into his head when they'd fixed him up. *Calls to a Crowded Room* continues to sell. He'll walk back in and Charlie will forgive him for almost setting the office on fire earlier today when he'd passed out and forgotten to take the tinfoil off of the easy-mac in the microwave. He'll forgive him for the errors he hasn't found in the manuscripts; he even managed to lose an entire document! Shultz had called the author back while spittle flew from his mouth. The manuscript had been used to wipe up a spill in the small kitchenette earlier this week, so it'd served some purpose. The file may or may not have been deleted from his computer. Shultz understands.

Remember the time you came home trashed at 4 am and I helped you puke into the sink and brought you breakfast the following morning Charlie, you fucking arrogant, exploitive asshole? Yeah, that's why you don't question my editing methods.

He'd almost sent that very text in an email earlier, but decided against it. Charlie would've laughed it off anyway, Charlie understands. Charlie

youlisten.youlisten.youlisten.youlisten.

is a great example of a professional connection and valued friend—no, *brother*. He's a *brother*, not a friend. And him? Stephen? Stephen's exceptional, a master editor, and Charlie's going to *die* when he sees this manuscript! It's coming along; the plot is completely laid out in his head, exactly the way he'd been laid up in his hospital bed after he'd been shot in the street. The look on Phoebe's face when he'd woken up? That *proves* these are all just ThOuGhTs! He knows she's completely faithful, and that the ajdskjfljges and fokewpojjoes of his mind are simply fjkasdjfiigjowe and jowejjojwing.

There's really not much more to it, is there? Nope, not at all. Not in the story of Stephen Christiansen, the author of *The Art of Falling*, *Trooper's Daughter* and *Calls to a Crowded Room*, Baltimore's own, the

all-American, the amazing, incredible, prodigious, miraculous, man-who-survived-being-shot, guy-who-would-be-on-Oprah-one-day
Hesavedmylife!HesavedmylifehoneyIKNOWthatguy!

Snapping back to consciousness like a faulty rubber band, Stephen barely prevents his head from crashing into the screen. Small stars appear as he rubs his eyelids, and he pulls his feet from the cluster of cans. *She's going to kill for me keeping the place like this.* His mind flashes back to a picture of them standing in a field of lights, him down on one knee, her soul bursting with joy as she jumped into his arms with the exclamation of all his hopes which have since died, moved out, abandoned him for larger houses and better men. Clicking around, he minimizes—for a moment!—the text of *the next great AMERICAN NOVEL* and pulls up his web browser. He types in the letters quickly, squinting. Hitting enter, he pulls up his Facebook to see his own picture smiling back at him.

They're together, standing at a benefit dinner for the publishing company. He's wearing a beautifully woven suit, a svelte, but dignified tie framing his dress shirt, his jacket bringing out his shoulders and accenting his clean-shaven face. His hand absently feels the scruffiness of his chin. His entire face is plucked and lithe with the accents of happiness; it'd only been three months ago. There'd been no reason to change his profile since then, solely the status quo of a waking reality haunted by the remnants of glory. He could easily turn the laptop's webcam on and witness his own visage in the descending pixels, but such would spoil the moment. His handsomeness in the image is off-set by the twinkling lighting of the banquet hall.

Attached to his left arm, filling up the other half of the picture, is a woman whose smile has brought him joy on the nights he's felt the most alone, who talked him through his tragedies and mended all his woes. Her hair is curled and flowing, the radiant burst of her oceanic irises offsetting her red coat. The picture is such that he can only see the two of them from the waist up, but he knows exactly how the rest of her looks. She's wearing a small necklace, which he knows somewhere in his mind was purchased in 2011 as an anniversary gift TheSameYearDadDied!WhatACoincidenceRight! and it still pales in comparison to the attractiveness of her face. Her dimples are shamelessly displayed. That's when laughing was easy. That's before he dreamed about her falling backwards or drifting away on a nightly basis, when the word *one* was a number instead of some insane flash bang grenade exploding in his sleep. Most importantly, he knows somewhere off-screen, at the end of one of that red coat's arms, is a hand which he's held a million times adorned with a ring which *proves* that dreams exists. It's irrefutable! He closes his profile picture's window and goes to chase more proof; he needs to convince *all* the doubters. They're a macabre bunch. He types the name *Phoebe Walker* into the search bar.

Her page pops up as the first result in the drop down menu, as if the Gods of the Internet have commanded it. Soon, she's looking back at him again, her profile picture a snapshot of the two of them together at a restaurant on an August date night. They'd been at a Hard Rock Cafe in the harbor and had felt compelled to document the meal. They're one of those couples who still goes on dates, even though they're irrevocably connected with no need for reminders; they go above and beyond, they're special, they do it because they *can* and because they *love* each other.

The words inflate his chest with surety and clarity; on her profile, it *clearly* states that she's engaged to Stephen Christiansen—it's been that way since they got their social media accounts. Their engagement is so strong that it actually pre-dates Facebook! How absolutely *awesome* that they've seen, since December 21st, 2006, two different Presidents in office, two and a half terms by Obama, seven different Super Bowls played, all three of his books published, the death of his father, and—he checks the calendar tab in the browser which keeps track of such fickle details—2,858 days of engagement. Oh, actually, now it's the 18th of October, so it's actually two-thousand eight-hundred and fifty *nine* days. That's obviously—including the day which just began, because today probably isn't the day they'll get married—68,616 hours, *approximately*, since he popped the question. That's *4,116,960* minutes since he pledged his heart and soul. Holy shit, what a number. It's only been 247,017,600 seconds—around— since she promised to build this life together with him. It's truly incredible that they've strengthened their bond over the years. They are a model story as to why people don't *need* to get married to be a married couple, and

I'm not ready. Next year looks a lot better. I want to get out of this town. I want us to build a house together, a real house, not an apartment, where we can raise a family. I want you to fly, and spread your wings, and become the amazing author I know you are, but I also know I'm not ready yet. I'm not ready. I'm not ready. I'm not ready. I'm not ready. I'm not ready. I'm not ready. I'm not ready. I'm not ready. I'm not ready. I'm not ready.

Clicking back to his news feed, he then returns to his profile. He knows what time it is. He goes and checks his recent activity, and then looks at his search history. The number is actually smaller, in terms of searches-per-hour, than yesterday. He's only searched for her thirty six times in the past six hours; that's only six per hour, to be fair. Yesterday, in the two hours he'd spent on a similar deluge, he'd searched for her 14 times, which is *seven* per hour. Feeling pleased with himself, Stephen closes his browser after deleting the history once again. He might die randomly from his bladder exploding due to all the iced tea, and that would be kind of embarrassing—his screen open in front of his lifeless body, with his search history on social media hiding only a couple of clicks away. That would be creepy, and probably would push her away from him a little bit more, even in death.

Oh right, the novel. He tabs back to the document on the bottom of his taskbar, labeled simply *the great American novel* to make sure people know what it is in case he spontaneously combusts, or the sleep deprivation caused by thegrassyknollonthehill causes him to step out into traffic, or take Dad's way out and shove a gun in his mouth and 'accidentally' pull the trigger. He isn't a pussy. Wrenching his train of thought back to his writing, he reviews the document to admire the work he's done so far:

It looks a little askew, he thinks. The white space needs to be primed a little bit more. He forgets exactly how far *behind schedule* he is. He's been preparing to write for the past few days; suddenly, he knows what it needs: *page numbers*. That'll make it almost a reward to actually get the amazing thoughts out of his mind.

He inserts page numbers, and a smile reaches his face as a blinking *1* now accents the blank page.

With that, he cracks open his 16th can of iced tea for the day, pleasures himself, and passes out.

(12)

"Stephen."

No response.

"Stephen."

A bird sings outside.

"*Stephen.*"

A rushing sensation smacks Stephen back to consciousness. His throat is barren, and both his arms—from being flattened under his weight—are numb. As he straightens out, the stiffness in his back aches in protest. Looking up, he groggily sees Phoebe standing at the edge of the couch, her face downcast.

"Hey, babe," He sits up, one of his arms supporting him like a pillar. The television is still on the same channel it'd been at midnight. Puzzled, he looks at the splash screen displaying the numbers 3:46. *It's not sunny at 3:46 in the morning*, Stephen thinks.

"Hi. How long have you been asleep for?" She asks. A barricade of iced tea cans, a dirty paper towel, copies of his novels, a manuscript, dirty dishes, his suit jacket, and one of the framed pictures from their bedroom prevents her from sitting down on the couch.

"A while, I think," He'd fallen asleep at well past midnight, and then woken up screaming at 4am. He'd swallowed another iced tea and dozed away again. It'd been the longest he'd slept all month.

"I see that," Phoebe's gaze both analyzes and cries out to him.

"What time did you get home?" Stephen asks, looking around him. *Oh my God, how much iced tea did I drink? How long was I awake?*

"Now. You didn't hear me walk in the door?" She asks, brushing crumbs from a snack Stephen ate off the arm of the couch.

"Nope, I was still out like a light."

"Why didn't you go to bed?"

"I was working on the novel."

"How far is it now?"

"Pretty far," Stephen says, coughing. He sits with his hands folded in his lap, the sleep unable to suppress his memories of the night.

"That's good to hear."

"How's Grace?"

"I wasn't at Grace's, remember?"

"Oh, right, yes, sorry," Stephen runs a hand across his greasy forehead.

"How are your friends doing?"

"Fine," Phoebe says. "I stayed over at Emily's house."

"Good. Did you guys have fun?"

"Ugh, Stephen," Phoebe says, knocking some of the cans off of the couch. The small apartment is pristine, save the island of self-immolation. "What is all of this? Where did you get this much iced tea?"

"I bought it in bulk," Stephen says. He picks up a half-empty bottle from the floor next to his feet and moves it to his lips. He stops himself before he drinks. Sniffing it, he realizes it's warm at the bottom instead of chilled, and smells mysteriously foul. Placing it back down, he shudders because he doesn't recall getting off the couch to use the restroom.

"What's gotten into you?" Phoebe asks, moving a plate away from her shoes.

"What do you mean?" Stephen asks, turning to face her. He picks up the remote from his workspace and turns off the television.

"Look at this. What in the hell? I know you've been hard at work on the novel, and I've tried to give you space to write, but ... this is disgusting. Is this what you've been doing when you haven't been coming to bed?"

"No," he lies. In the past month, she's turned in well before him. The shooting had been the first week of September, and the visions since then have evolved, along with the sinking feeling of his stomach's lining being removed by an unseen hand.

"Then what is it? Are you feeling depressed again?" Her voice is pained. She sets her purse down and crosses her arms.

"Nah, it's not that. I've been extremely focused on this novel."

"Don't lie to me," Phoebe's voice is small.

"I'm not lying to you," Stephen brushes his dress pants, stained orange and spotted with an ungodly collage of substances.

"Can I see how much you have, then?" Phoebe asks.

"Why are you being so invasive?" Stephen snaps. The computer sits between the two of them silently, a child in an argument.

Phoebe does a double take. "What? Invasive? Stephen, you're literally working on this every waking hour you can. I haven't spoken to you in the past two days."

"That's because you've been out of the house a lot. I've been here the entire time."

"I've tried talking to you to get you to move off of this. You've been like this since the shooting."

"The shooting?" Stephen looks down at his left shoulder and moves it carefully. It only evokes a whisper of discomfort. "I think I'm fine, I think you're reading too much into me working hard on this novel."

"Then I'm happy for you. Why won't you let us both be happy and let me see it?"

"I'll show you it if you want," Stephen says. He moves in front of the computer, and types in his password as prompted. Before he can go any further, Phoebe leans in and sees what's on the tab.

"What is that?" She asks. Stephen attempts to move the cursor to the word document cued at the bottom, but stops when she touches his hand. He sits back and lets her see the screen.

"Wedding venues?" She says. "Is this my Facebook? Are you serious?"

Shrugging, Stephen says, "I've been looking at wedding venues."

"For what?"

"A wedding."

Pushing his hand out of the way, Phoebe moves to the Word document. After clicking it, she turns to Stephen once more, her mouth set into a discerning grimace.

"There's nothing here," She says, moving the scrollbar up and down on the screen. "Steve, there is nothing in this document."

"Wrong," Stephen says. "There's page numbers!"

"Stephen, where is the novel?"

"That is the novel, Phoebe."

"What? What the fuck do you mean this is the novel? There's literally nothing here!"

Raising his hands as if Phoebe's the one who shot him, Stephen says, "It's coming to me. I've been doing a lot of brainstorming."

"Have you been looking at wedding venues and daydreaming this entire time?"

"Daydreaming?" Stephen says, and now the coiled feelings which have haunted him rise to the surface; the banality of his tone vanishes. "Is that what you call this? Daydreaming?"

"You've been fantasizing about God knows what when you said you've been working."

"I've been thinking of what it would be like if we were married, yes."

"Oh my God."

"What, Phoebe? What?"

"What are those numbers in the search bar?" She moves from tab to tab, each number on the screen increasing as she goes.

"Nothing."

"Bullshit."

"They're my book sales," Stephen coughs.

"That's a lie. You haven't sold ... what, 3 million books?"

"How would you know? You haven't asked me about the sales in months."

"What? Stephen, why are you so angry with me?" Phoebe shifts back to her side of the couch.

The snap of the laptop closing accompanies a hollow laugh from Stephen. No humor lingers in the air. "I'm not angry with you. I just don't understand."

"Understand what?"

"Why the fuck you won't marry me."

"What? We've been over this a million times."

"Yeah, and you don't give a damn how much it hurts me," Stephen yells. Phoebe flinches at Stephen's quick ferocity. "You keep finding reason after reason to say no. I keep saying I'll do *anything* to be able to call you my wife. I made a promise to you, and you promised to me, that we were in this together. How many people do you know who wait what, seven, eight years to actually commit to one another?"

"I've always been committed to you."

"Bullshit! That's fucking bullshit!" Stephen smacks the couch cushion with a closed fist.

His outburst bounces off Phoebe like an unexploded bomb.

"People don't wait for the perfect time," Stephen snarls. "They plan as they go along. We've been sitting in stagnation for the past seven years in this god damn apartment after we graduated from college and moved into the city, after you finished your training, after I started Bessemer with Charlie, and you keep saying how much you hate it, and how much you want a family, and I've said, time and time again, that I will do *anything* to make you happy, Phoebe. That's all I've ever wanted to do."

"No," Phoebe says, shaking her head.

"No? What do you mean 'no'?"

"You're fine with the way things are. You're content with me going to work endlessly in a city I didn't originally want to stay in until you founded Bessemer. I moved with you. I support your dreams, and you supported mine too, to a point, but then it became apparent what you truly love."

"What?" Stephen throws his arms up, as if he's pandering to an audience. "What are you talking about? I love you, I've always loved you."

"No, you're engaged to your career. The tours you do, the amount of time you spend at work editing, refining—you've always wanted this, but it's not conducive to marriage. You love your books more than me."

Taking a couple seconds to mull her words over, Stephen treats them as if he's trying to discern the flavor of a chewy candy. A verdict reaches him.

"Are you fucking insane?" Stephen asks.

"No, I'm not *fucking insane*, I'm hurt!" Phoebe stands, her voice rising to levels Stephen hasn't heard in years.

"You selfish bastard, this is exactly what I'm talking about. You spend your time focused on climbing ladders, and you make it seem like you take my feelings into account. You take me around to all of your gatherings, your events, and you would *love* to be able to say I'm your wife so you can show everyone exactly how much you've gotten your life back together. You're obsessed with confirming the two of us because that's how you show you've changed from being who you were before. You're motivated by advancing your own self-interest."

"So, you don't want me to focus on my career?" Stephen rises to match her, his voice emotional but controlled. "You'd rather I what, drop it all and run back to Pennsylvania like we're 21 again, without any ties or obligations?"

Phoebe's face contorts into a grimace, her teeth gritting. She doesn't respond.

"I can't forget everything to move somewhere else. Charlie relies on me. I agree, this house isn't big enough for a family, but we could buy outside of Carbondale. You say where, and I'll go. You're right, I don't mind things as they are now, and I honestly don't see a reason why you can't commit to us."

"That's the problem," Phoebe's voice is deafeningly calm. "You only see what you want to see, only feel what you want to feel, only do what you want to do. I'm along for the ride. A marriage is supposed to be a partnership, a mutual build, a mutual --"

"How have I not made our relationship exactly that, baby?" Stephen takes a step closer to her, and she backs away. He stops, and she stands her ground. The distance between them is only a few feet, but holds the length of years.

"Don't call me baby," Phoebe says.

"If you were so dissatisfied with this life of ours, why didn't you bring it up? Why did you never try and talk to me about this?" Stephen asks.

"I have, I've been ignored because you're so obsessed with getting married."

"Uhm, Phoebe, you promised to marry me. That's why we got engaged."

"I didn't promise to marry you," She says. "21 year old Phoebe Walker promised to marry you; I'm 28 year old Phoebe Walker. You don't know me. You know me as you want to know me, you know the girl who was head over heels in love with you since sophomore year of college, when she was 19 and you took her virginity, promised her the world, and then subjugated her to being a supporting actress in your movie over the next seven years. We don't sleep together anymore; you're obsessed with me, apparently, and you wake up after dreaming about me, all because you won't listen to me and I won't agree to lock myself to this life which is stagnant for me, and vibrant for you."

"I always wanted to build this life for both of us," Stephen's voice grows soft.

"You're lying," Phoebe says, her arms crossed. She's wearing the same red jacket she'd worn to the banquet in the Facebook pictures.

"I'm not lying. Why don't you believe me?"

"Actions speak louder than words, Stephen. You love your books, you --"

"I DEDICATED THEM TO YOU!" Stephen roars, kicking a pair of iced tea cans from the floor. "I put my heart and soul into these books to make them gifts for the people I love! You're my world, Phoebe!" Now his demeanor breaks, and the tears come. "You're my fucking world. I would die for you. I'll give up everything I have, I'll stop writing, and I'll leave Bessemer, to make you happy." He walks forward, and this time she doesn't back away. He takes her hands in his, and he looks straight at her.

"I would do anything for you. I'm sorry I haven't listened. We can sell this place, we have more than enough money to upgrade. We're four, five, six years overdue. We can buy a house in any state you want. I'll write from there, we'll start over again. We'll be a fresh couple, can get married, and bury this shit behind us."

Before he can continue, Phoebe rips her hands from his and steps away to observe him in full. His hair resembles scruff and tear, his shirt is spotted, his dress pants soiled, his face unshaven and red, a bit of snot leaking from his nose.

"I never said you didn't love me."

Her words hang in the air, and for a moment she's 19 again. He blinks, and she's the 22 year old, the 25 year old, his fiancée, his world, his darling, his everything.

"What do you want to say to me, Phoebe?"

Her face breaks, and the tears rain down. Her shoulders are rivets in an earthquake, and her makeup runs like black rivers.

Stephen steps forward and attempts to hug her, but she pushes him away. He tries again, and she moves out of his reach once more. He's crying as hard as she is.

Sputtering, she regains her composure. Her back is facing the front door. The sunlight of the windows bounces off her hair; she's absolutely gorgeous.

"Stephen," she says. He looks at her, and they seem to stand as moments in time. "I'm past you."

Reaching his ears, the words don't register meaning. The bullet's impact had a similar effect, one wherein his body obviously received the blow, but his conscious mind was too numb to comprehend. In a parallel fashion, Phoebe's revelation pierces his chest and collides with his heart so hard he actually ceases breathing for a moment. The only syllable which escapes is feeble.

"What?"

"It's the truth. I don't love you," She sniffles, and she's calm.

"What does that mean, Phoebe?"

"We're not getting married. We're not going to build a life together."

"Why?" Stephen asks, and he feels rage. He's fucked it all up and lost the only thing which really matters to him. All of the compounded mistakes he's made over the years of their relationship flush into his consciousness, and the s from the dam of his broken soul rush out. He sobs harder than he had at the news of his father's suicide, at the news of his mother's death, at any rejection letters he'd gotten from publishers or the unpredictability of such a cruel world. The images in his head which he's dreamed of since the age of 19 all catch ablaze, and he's on his knees of the apartment where love was made, love was treasured, and now love dies.

"I'm sorry." Phoebe says. She doesn't move, she doesn't cry, and she doesn't comfort her fallen fiancé. The scene which played out in the darkest corners of her mind now manifests itself into the world.

Two minutes pass, and she walks past him into the bedroom they've shared. She grabs a bag, enough to last her until she comes back to clean out the rest. She ignores the pictures on the wall as she puts the blouses, shirts, and pants which he's seen her wear so many times into the bag. She takes her perfume, her toothbrush, another pair of shoes, and a couple childhood mementos and tucks them away. Walking back into the living room, it's as if the hours she's spent in the apartment line up in an ungodly procession.

Remaining on the floor, Stephen doesn't look at her. She walks near the door, stopping to kneel down with him.

"Stephen," she says softly. "Look at me."

His ruined face might as well be a church whose religion is extinct.

"Stephen."

Finally, he raises his head, and his expression stabs her.

"I want you to move past me. I want you to go out there and conquer the world like you've always wanted. You're an amazing author."

The following glance from Stephen reaches deep inside of her, to the fiber of her being. Chills reverberate down Phoebe's back.

Stephen shows a smile, which turns into a grin as he shakes his head.

The sobs of earlier, and the screaming, have ruined his voice, but it doesn't matter. The death knell of their future freezes the air.

"Always and forever plus one, right?"

Phoebe can't stop the onslaught, and she's broken now, crying harder than she's ever cried before.

Now Stephen's emotions choke out his voice. He shudders into the carpet, gasping. Phoebe gets up, covering her face, and rushes out the door, the wooden frame with the number of their apartment, 48, slamming behind her.

Inside one of the covers of *Calls to a Crowded Room* on the couch, these words are written:

Dedicated to Phoebe, the love of my life. All of my work would be
impossible without your love and support.
You are my world.

[13]

The door to Alfie's swings open brusquely. Today, the television sets' hum does not draw the eye of Isaac Sellers. He scans the tables where he'd eaten with Stephen before, and finds a different man: a disheveled form sitting at the end of the bar, three seats away from the other patrons. He's a caricature resembling Isaac's mental image, but distorted, as if morphed by a cartoonist's brush. Odd ends have been added to the portrait, including a tall glass of golden liquid waiting on the counter. His jacket drapes his shoulders, but the t-shirt he's wearing underneath no longer aspires to professionalism. Lastly, he reacts to the Ravens-Falcons game on television similarly to the other men at the bar. Among the throng, yet removed, it would be impossible to tell Stephen as any different from the men cheering and jeering at the orchestration of the sports.

Taking another swig of alcohol, Stephen notices Isaac drifting across the bar. The beer sloshes over the side of the glass, the remnants a waterfall down to the wood.

"Isaac! My man!" Stephen pats Isaac on the back of his jacket. Isaac stops for a moment, before taking the seat next to Stephen and folding his hands.

"Hello, Stephen. I'm glad you asked me to have lunch today."

"Of course! Man, you're one of my best friends, you know that?" Stephen punctuates his sentence with another dip in the drink.

"Thanks," Isaac examines Stephen as Stephen turns back to the screen. Stephen notices his cup is empty.

"Kelly!" he calls. "Kelly, I need a refill!" The patrons behind them enjoying their more traditional dinners—ones involving solid food instead of straight booze—glance quickly at him, but then return to their meals. The group of men to Isaac's left remains undisturbed in their bubble of chatter.

The bartender, a girl in her mid-20's with her hair pinned back and an accepting grimace, walks over to Stephen before he can yell again.

"Kelly, darling, can you please buy my buddy Isaac here a drink? And can I get another refill? You can put his on my tab," Stephen leans in as he gives the order, patting Isaac on the shoulder again.

"No, I mean, uhm, sorry," Isaac interjects. Kelly raises an eyebrow "I'd much prefer a water if you don't mind."

"Really?" Stephen asks, his emotions drawn out and soaked. His breath hits Isaac's nostrils in a pungent cloud. "You don't want a beer? Come on, to watch the game? You drink, don't you?"

"No, not anymore," Isaac says, offering an apologetic signal to the bartender. Shrugging, she refills Stephen's glass.

"That's a shame, man. I'd been holding off since my college days, it's like I'm backlogged or some shit, I need to make up for lost time," Stephen laughs, and thanks Kelly for the drink. In a gulp, he's gone through a quarter of the glass.

"I didn't know you drank," Isaac says, leaning on his folded arms.

"I didn't, until today." Stephen says. The crowd reacts to a burst of cheering from the television. Isaac remains stoic.

"How many beers is this?" Isaac asks.

"Uhhhhh," Stephen responds. "I'm unsure, we'll have to ask Kelly when she gets back. Kelly!" Stephen's voice whips through the restaurant again. Hurriedly, the bartender returns with Isaac's glass of water. Isaac nods and thanks her, and Stephen poses the question to her. She stops, counting for a moment, and eventually says he's had 8 beers over the course of the hour. Isaac turns, his expression aghast, as she walks back to the other side of the bar.

"God, she has a nice ass," Stephen watches her leave.

"Mr. Christiansen," Isaac's posture is no longer relaxed. "What is ... what is wrong with you?"

"Nothing!" Stephen replies, shaking his head dismissively. "Absolutely nothing! What makes you ask?"

"You've had nine beers in sixty minutes and complimented the bartender in a not very platonic fashion."

"And?" Stephen drinks again. "Is a man not allowed to look?"

"I don't know. What about Phoebe?"

At the mention of her name, Stephen throws his head back and drains his drink. The liquid rushes down his throat. Stephen wipes his face and plants the glass firmly on the bar, his knuckles white. He turns to Isaac, his face a morgue of emotions.

"What about her?"

Stepping back, Isaac holds up his hands the same way he had during the robbery.

"I'm sorry I asked. Did something happen?"

"No, no, not at all," Stephen says, looking into the glass like a telescope. "Nope, Phoebe's fine, she's completely fine. Fine!" The alcohol is not enough to weaken the 1000 proof sarcasm.

"Did you two have a fight?"

"Yeah," Stephen says nonchalantly. "You could say that."

"What happened, if you don't mind me asking?"

"Oh," Stephen makes a pushing motion with his hand. "Nothing really big happened. She's upset; she's probably going to spend a couple days at her sister Grace's house. She's been seeing Grace a lot lately, plus her friends Emily and Jessica too, plus some other really hot friend named Vicky. I'm telling you bro, if I wasn't engaged ..."

"Stephen, stop," Isaac says, grabbing Stephen's arm.

"What?" Stephen's replies. "Isn't a man allowed to notice beauty?"

"What caused her to move out?"

"No, no, no, no. No," Stephen puts his hands in front of Isaac, a professor correcting a student. "She didn't move out. All she did was pack a bag and tell me she doesn't love me anymore."

The color rushes out of Isaac's face. "What? What made her say that?"

"She thinks that I've been ignoring her, and that she's changed, and something about how she didn't see enough people before agreeing to marry me. We talked it over last night after she left, she eventually picked up after I called her enough. Kelly!" Stephen beckons to the bartender.

"How many times did you call her?" Isaac asks as the bartender refills Stephen's glass.

"Not that many, only like ten, maybe fifteen?"

"In one night?"

"Hey man," Stephen chuckles a tad, his eyeballs glazed. "It's not as bad as when she was out and I searched her on Facebook. One night I searched for her *thirty six times in six hours*, so we're already getting better."

"Oh my God." Isaac recoils as the beer arrives expediently. Stephen drowns himself willingly. He burps, a painful noise followed by a breath.

"Man … I'm worried about … us, you know? You know you have those parts in your relationship, those days where doubt seems a little more … prevalent than your vows? I think this entire weekend has been one of those days. She'll come around eventually; she agreed to marry me for a reason, you know?"

"I … I hate to be a downer, Stephen, but … it sounds like she meant to move out instead of leave for a couple days," Isaac says sheepishly.

"Pssssh, Isaac, my brother … bro." Stephen chuckles. "You, you're my bro." He laughs harder, draping an arm around Isaac's shoulders. "You know … you're the first black friend I've ever had, you know that?"

Shimmying uncomfortably, Isaac says, "Gee, uh … the honor is mine."

"No, no, no no no, the honor is truly *mine*. I had a couple appliances … no, assoshit—associat—acquaint fences, right, in college who were upstanding, strong, independent black men."

A short, nervous burst escapes Isaac's lips. "Jesus, I don't know if I should be crying at this or laughing."

"What's there to cry about nowadays?" Stephen asks, his trusty beer in hand. "I got everything I need. I have great company, great atmosphere, I got my bro, I'm … I'm an *author*!" Stephen shakes Isaac, who almost falls off his stool.

"Why wouldn't Phoebe be completely in love with me?" Stephen continues. "She's … having some personal issues right now, and once they're sorted out, everything will be *perfecto*!" He drains the glass, and bellows "KELLY!" across the bar.

"Hey, asshole, can you keep it down a bit?" A man at the opposite end of the bar yells at Stephen. Stephen turns in his direction, and flips him off. Isaac mutters "oh no" under his breath and releases himself from Stephen's embrace.

"Hey man, chill out, I'm trying to enjoy the show!" Stephen's using his hands as if he's giving an invisible puppet show.

"Yeah, well, you're acting like a dick and yelling over the game!"

"Hey," Stephen screams back, standing. His mood downshifts like a car going up a hill, strained and vocal. "Don't you call me a dick, you fuckhead!"

"What the hell? What is with you?" The patron yells back.

"You heard me asshole, don't you start shit with me," Stephen picks up the next beer Kelly gives him. Behind the bar, she's doing her best impersonation of a bottle on the shelf as the two men exchange words. The man opposite Stephen is a burly biker, perhaps in his mid-thirties, and he's standing too.

"What's the matter with you? Don't you have any manners?" the man asks.

"What's the matter with me?" Stephen responds, his voice a

crescendo. Isaac's heart pounds inside his jacket as he attempts to watch the game. The Ravens are kicking ass, and hopefully Stephen isn't the next victim.

"Nothing's the matter with me. What's the matter with you? I'm great, I'm awesome, I'm ready to go home to my fiancée."

"That'll be tough to do," the guy responds, his tone imbued with wit.

"And why do you say that?" Stephen's grip tightens around the glass. His face riddles with confusion.

"She'll be at my place for the night riding my cock," The guy grins, revealing a row of chipped, yellow teeth.

Stephen raises the glass above his head and slams it down on the counter like a falling boulder. The customers enjoying their dinners all gasp as the glass shatters, the alcohol and a bit of Stephen's blood cascading across the wood like a breaking wave. Isaac's arms instinctively grab Stephen as he attempts to lurch towards the man at the end of the bar. The man's friends, also seemingly members of the Nice Biker Club of Baltimore, are all laughing as Isaac restrains a struggling Stephen with palpable—yet relatively simple—effort.

"FUCK YOU MOTHERFUCKER, YOU WANT TO TALK ABOUT MY FIANCÉE LIKE THAT I'LL SHOW YOU HOW TO RIDE A DICK! I'LL RIDE YOUR DICK SO HARD YOU WON'T BE ABLE TO FEEL IT IN THE MORNING YOU BABY BACK BITCH!"

The bikers have descended into a squall of laughter, the instigator clutching his chest in guffaws.

"Stephen, Stephen, Steeephen," Isaac's voice flexes as he drags Stephen back to his seat, which is now splattered in honey colored fluid tinged with red.

"What? Did you hear what that shithead said to me? I'll strangle him if he goes anywhere near my fiancée."

"Stephen, calm down. I want you to count to ten --" Isaac's advice is broken up by the arrival of the manager from the kitchen. A balding man at the mid-life crisis age, he quietly walks up to Stephen as the ambiance of the room returns to calm.

"Sir, I'm going to need to ask you to pay and leave," The manager says. He's a good head shorter than Isaac and Stephen.

"Ok, thank you, sir, we'll be on our way," Isaac gently says, still clutching Stephen by the arm. "Pay, Stephen."

Still fuming, Stephen reaches into his pocket. He counts out forty dollars, and leaves it on the top of the bar, letting it float in the alcohol next to Kelly.

"Keep the change, thank you," Isaac shakes the manager's hand with his free arm. "Walk," he hisses at Stephen.

The manager steps aside as Isaac leads Stephen past the group of bikers to the door. Stephen's shoes squeak across the floor.

"Have fun riding his dick, sweetheart!" one of the bikers calls as they leave.

"Yes, thank you—keep walking." Isaac says, half to the biker, half to Stephen. Stephen tries to stop, but Isaac pushes him out into the waning fall afternoon. The bikers shake their heads and return to the game. Five minutes later, they'll cheer as the Ravens score, the entire scene forgotten.

They find a small bench near the curb, a block or two away from the eatery. Stephen flexes his right hand, feeling the small cuts expand and retract. Isaac sits with his arms folded between his knees. Neither speak, with Stephen panting and Isaac staring at the passing cars. A few minutes pass, and Isaac's attention turns to Stephen when he hears him crying into his cut hands, the tears swimming around the cracks in his skin.

Saying nothing, Isaac places an arm around Stephen's shoulders, and pats him gently. Stephen's simple tears turn into sobs, and soon into aches of his soul. Their shadows are adjacent on the cement behind them, their silhouettes meshing.

The Baltimore sun descends in the sky, an audience to the two men together. It will, over the course of the next twenty minutes, see the two men rise from that bench, Isaac guiding Stephen like a fire signal on a gray morning, eventually going to his own car and driving Stephen home to his apartment. Isaac will take Stephen's keys, and he and his wife Olivia will drive back to bring Stephen's car home in the same night. Stephen won't remember how hard he hugs Isaac at the end of the day, or the depth of his sleep that night, but part of his completely broken person is pushed a little back together by the benevolent arms of a genuine friend.

[14]

The hill's gone now; all the grass is dead, paved over and made into a parking lot for a local mall. Stephen stands in the center, the pavement barren. The white lines extend to forever; the sky is blue and bright overhead; a couple of birds fly in the distance.

Stephen jerks into awareness, an inverse lucidity; he knows he's dreaming, and he wants nothing more than to stay in the dream. His mind is split, because inside the dream he's aware he's dreaming, but his brain, bushwhacked and fragmented by the alcohol, holds him in slumber. Grassy knolls, he knows, only exist in worlds where lovers are perfect. There is an extent to vows which claim forever and ever, and a use-by date for an engagement ring. The world is constantly changing, revolving, evolving, turning, spinning; the fate of the universe lies in the weight of a single moment.

Surveying the parking lot, Stephen takes a step forward; the ground seems to move, but he knows he's stationary. His feet stay in place; it's the earth turning underneath him instead of his legs. The white lines shift in their constant pattern, bouncing in and out of his peripheral vision. A slight breeze sweeps the land, embracing him with the smell of her perfume. There are suddenly seven birds; they swoop down to encircle his head, twittering. Stephen strains his ears, and he can hear their singsong mutterings forming the patterns into sense:

"I don't love you anymore, I don't love you anymore!"

The syllables transfix him, his hands following the traces of their wings. He takes a swipe and tries to catch one, but they're holographic. His mind is a watershed of alcohol and corrupted love, which sleep can numb but never heal. He keeps swatting at the birds, until they fly upwards, ascending on the current of his sluggish breath. He blows a gust of air, and the birds circle faster and faster, conjoining and disappearing with a poof into the ethers of his mind. He shakes his head, befuddled momentarily like a disconnected controller. A voice cracks through the beauty of the stillness, calling "Stephen Christiansen!", and he turns.

Around 10 feet from him stands a man wearing a brown jacket and matching slacks, with a grand beard of white covering his face. His pocket is a pouch for pens, and his face home to a grandfatherly smile. A large black chalkboard on rolling wheel sits to his immediate left. For some reason, he's shirtless, and curly white chest hair lines the space between the two folds of his jacket as if it's a batch of coiled tinsel from last year's Christmas tree.

"Dr. Fonz?" Stephen asks.

The old man chuckles in delight, and waves the yardstick in his hand.

"Ah, so you do remember me, Stephen my boy! Stephen, son of Christian," The old man winks, and Stephen smiles.

"What are you doing here, Dr. Fonz?"

"Shhhhh," The old man says, holding a finger to his lips. Stephen doesn't remember his nipples being so round. "We don't want to disturb the others in class."

"Class? What class?" Stephen asks, looking around.

"My class, silly boy! We're in Numbers and Real World Applications again!"

"We are?" Stephen's eyebrows rise, and suddenly he's missing his calculator, his backpack, his notebook, and—oh shit—he forgot his protractor!

"Don't look so discouraged, Stephen. You're the only student here today. I was pulling your leg!"

"Oh, thank goodness," Stephen relaxes.

"You're the only one who enrolled. Everyone else stopped coming to my classes after my heart attack in 2010. What a way to go out, right?"

"Oh, yeah, I remember that," Stephen suddenly remembers the text of an alumni email from his campus registry reporting Dr. Fonz's untimely passing.

"Of course you do, Stevie. You were always one of my favorites."

"Thank you, Dr. Fonz. I always enjoyed your class."

"Why, you must've! Now, let's get started with today's lesson, shall we?"

"Of course," Stephen says. He sits at the desk which appears next to him.

"So, numbers, yes?" Dr. Fonz says, removing a pair of eyeglasses from inside his jacket. *"Funny little things they are. Really, they're marks on a paper which we humans were smart enough—or stupid enough—to give meaning,"* The old man reaches up and spins the chalkboard to the opposite side, revealing a collection of scrambled numbers of varying sizes.

"Explicitly, this garble means nothing. There's a 70 here," he circles a spot on the blackboard. *"A 69 here,"* another circle. *"A 48 here, a 13 here, but they don't exactly mean much at all, correct?"* His question hangs in the air, and Stephen nods.

Flipping the chalkboard again, a solitary number now stands out in the blackness.

"Now, what does this number say, Stephen?"

"28," Stephen answers.

"Why is this number important? What meaning does it have?"

"It's ... my age?" Stephen asks warily.

"Good! Yes, your age," Dr. Fonz gives a thumbs up.

Flipping the board again, the collage of numbers has morphed into a single 36.

"Now, what does this number represent?"

Confounded, Stephen places his chin on his palm.

"I don't know," Stephen says.

"Here, this might help." Dr. Fonz's chalk is fast over the well-used blackboard. *"Sometimes, numbers have even greater meanings, or only have meanings at all, when placed in connection with other numbers. Now can you tell me what these are equal to?"*

The board now displays 36 + 14.

His left hand tapping the desk in a small drumbeat, Stephen still can't decode the cryptograph of simple math.

"I still don't know, Dr. Fonz. I'm sorry, I haven't done math in a while."

"It's quite alright, Stephen. No worries!" he draws an = 50 to solve the problem. "This represents the number of times you searched for your ex-fiancée's name on Facebook before she left you. I understand why it might be complex, it's quite alright."

His neck freezes as if it's been pelted by frozen rain. "Did I really?"

"Hm? Yes?" Dr. Fonz responds, about to flip the board again. "Did you really what?"

"Sit there like a loser plugging her into Facebook?"

"Oh, well, that leads me to the next number, as a matter of fact!" Dr. Fonz spins the board, and another equation has materialized: 19 + 9 = ?

"How about this equation, Stephen?"

"I don't know," Stephen's face is flush.

"Well, one way to solve an equation is to first find the value of each number," He circles the 19, and then taps it with the yardstick.

"That's how many Arnold Palmer iced teas—strawberry, might I add—you consumed last Friday night. It's as if you were trying to give yourself diabetes!" He flashes a grin, then circles the next number. "That term—9—is how many beers you had last night before your friend had to drive you home to your apartment."

He fills in the rest of the equation.

"Now, we have this number, 28." Dr. Fonz taps the chalk. "28 is a very interesting number. To crack its code, we must, as the kids said in my last lecture before my untimely demise, 'go deeper.'"

His palms clammy, Stephen watches.

"Let's do this: let's divide the 28 by four. Do you know why we're dividing it by 4, Stephen?"

"No," Stephen replies.

"Ah! Well, that's how many times you've seriously considered suicide

over the course of your life; once after your mother passed when you were 16, once again when you were 17, for a short moment after your father's bull's-eye to his own brain via his mouth, and, of course, your current circumstance," Dr. Fonz makes a gun with his finger and puts it next to his head, indenting his thumb as if to pull the trigger.

"So, if we work it out," Dr. Fonz's chalk skates across the board. "We determine that 28 divided by four equals 7. Now, this number is a little bit off, and we are making a conscious rounding error," Dr. Fonz explains. Stephen can feel the blood pounding in his ears.

"See, we can't round this 7 to an 8, because the 7 is technically how many years you were engaged—past tense—to your fiancée. While December is only two months away, the two of you are no longer together, so we have to call it 7. I don't want to deal in decimals, so we're being rebels and taking this juicy whole number 7 and discarding the equivalent of the last 10 months. Do you follow?"

Stephen nods.

"Great! Excellent, you get a gold star. We're almost at the end of our sequence! One more step to go," He flips the board once more, and one final equation remains:

$7 - 6 = ?$

"So, Stephen, apply what we've learned so far. Break it down piece by piece, I know you can do it even though you were an English major. The Core was a requirement for a reason!" He grins with his pearly, gapped teeth.

"Alright," Stephen says. "The seven is how many years I was engaged."

"Great start!" Dr. Fonz claps excitedly. "The tense is correct! Of course it is, you author you."

"And the six ..."

"Actually, you wouldn't know this part. I'm sorry," Dr. Fonz shakes his head angrily. "I didn't give you enough information."

He draws a circle around the six, and then points to Stephen.

"This is how many years your relationship was monogamous."

The seditious symbols all cascade out of the sky, drifting into sense *miraculously.*

"Don't worry, don't worry," Dr. Fonz continues. "It was my mistake. Us teachers mess up too, sometimes."

"What do you mean monogamous?"

"Dammit, Stevie, I thought you were a writer! It means your fiancée started cheating on you around two years ago."

Leaning back in his chair, Stephen desires nothing more than for the legs to snap so he could shatter his brain all over the parking lot.

"Don't fret, my boy, don't fret," Dr. Fonz consoles him. "You'll remember none of this when you wake up. I'll be dead and buried, along with all the emotions you've been drowning in for the past month. See! I used a complex verb, 'drowning', in order to convey how much of a shithead you are!" Dr. Fonz's guffaws race across the empty parking lot. "Are you proud of me, Stevie? Are you, you worthless piece of human garbage?" He slaps his knee.

Expressionless, a sensation of floating turns Stephen's muscles to putty.

"Oh, yes, the final part of this equation is the most important," Dr. Fonz turns the board over a final time, and a huge 1 is displayed in rainbow colored chalk.

"This is the number one, Stephen. It's the loneliest number, but also the most important number which you shall remember for the rest of your life."

Stephen coughs.

"Taking six away from seven, you're left with one," Dr. Fonz holds up one finger.

Churning, Stephen's stomach boils in protest, causing him to cough harder.

"Your homework is to simply wait and see what this number means. You've waited your entire life for what is coming to you. You've dreamt about it all this month," Dr. Fonz's face turns dark, and his voice loses its cheer like a deflating blow-up snowman. He's Santa Claus if Santa played a Hitchcock villain.

"And it's coming to you, Stephen," He's standing over Stephen now,

blocking out the sun. The chalkboard spins in constant rotations, pieces of chalk scattering across the open parking lot. The birds return as airborne ravens, screaming "I DON'T LOVE YOU ANYMORE!"

Coughing his lungs out, Stephen hunches over the cold plastic of the desk.

"ONE!" Dr. Fonz bellows, snapping the yardstick. "ONE! ONE!" He pushes Stephen out of his seat. The sky darkens. The rains come. A crossroad. She's down the right path, drifting away. "ONE!" Torrential rain pours down on the parking lot. He's coughing so hard it feels like his throat is aflame. Through the cyclone, Dr. Fonz, his veins bulging, his eyes popping, screams, "THERE IS A GRASSY KNOLL ON A HILL!"

The breathing stops, and the world goes white.

Crashing through the floor of sleep, Stephen's throat is like hot tar. The remnants from the night shoot across his bed. Isaac had left him lying on his side; the torrents of alcohol are coughed up in a horridly foul fluid, which ruins the pristine bed he used to share. After nearly all of the contents of his stomach are expelled, his abdomen is a ball of heat. The smell reaches his nostrils and he feels as if he's going to die. A drumbeat of the hangover rings in his ears, smashing down his temples in force. After breathing in agony for a few moments, he turns to observe the clock. 5:50. Is it Saturday? That's the day she left. Sunday. Sunday was when he went to Alfie's. She hadn't called him on Sunday. *Monday?* He has work. He can't miss a day. He'll be fired.

He moves, his vomit stained shirt, mixing with the sweat from the night, sticking like demented latex on his chest. He staggers, and holds onto the wall for support, and knocks down a picture which had been hanging there, of a young couple standing with the Baltimore harbor in the background. It clatters to the floor, and Stephen feels the Yosemite of his stomach cocking its barrels. Rushing to the bathroom, he kneels in front of the toilet, a voice in his mind whispering the word "one."

[15]

Charlie Shultz's office is larger than Stephen's, sitting a few doors down the halls of Bessemer Press. The rectangular shape of the building betrays an interior which is quite intimate. Scrawled on the door in a vibrant and curvy font are the words *Director Charles Shultz*. However, a few of those who have been around for Bessemer's five year existence are aware of a man underneath the grandiose titles and the passionate persona.

Sitting behind his simple desk, Shultz's hands do not punctuate every sentence he speaks; instead, they lay resigned, with their fingers poised to dig into the wood. A jacket does not flow from his arms and cast shadows onto his back; it hangs from the chair in which he sits. The rows of bookcases to his left hold works from Bessemer's history and also his personal favorites, and the huge glass window behind him looks out to the streets of Baltimore. Usually, in his free time, he'd peruse these different sections of his niche in the world.

Today, he's focused on the figure who slumps in front of him, and his usually decedent smile is a grimaced line. He knows the man sitting in the chair is one of the few who remain at the Press who know him not as Director Charles Shultz, but Charlie. The combined weight of the history now thickens the air in the room.

"I don't know what to say," Shultz murmurs, adjusting his crimson tie.

Rubbing his forearms gently, Stephen says nothing.

"I honestly don't. As your boss, as your friend, as a brother, I'm lost for words," Shultz continues.

The very air which Stephen inhales bears a weight; his eyes are bloodshot, his hair still wet from the morning shower. The clock on Shultz's desk displays 8:45, 45 minutes after opening.

"I refuse to believe it. Ever since you and Phoebe met, I've seen firsthand how much she cares for you."

Despite the soreness of his mouth, Stephen's laugh is like "Taps" at a military funeral.

"That was seven years ago, Charlie," his voice is a concerto of hoarseness, coarseness, and gloom. "Seven years ago, I knew how much she loved me. It's actually almost eight years. Well, it *was* almost eight years. Over those eight years we reached some amazing heights together, turned our thoughts into ambition. I dedicated books to her, I told her all the time how much I loved her and appreciated her. She became as necessary to me as the air I breathed every day, and all it's gotten me now is this," Stephen shrugs, his shoulders sagging.

"Don't talk like that," Shultz leans across his desk, past a picture of him and his own wife. "Don't do that to yourself. She'll come around."

"Charlie," Stephen interjects. Shultz over-talks him.

"She'll realize what she's doing is wrong, she'll talk it out, she'll come back."

"Charlie," Stephen's voice rises.

"I know her and you very well, she's going to-"

"Charlie!" Stephen's voice breaks, and now he hunches with his face in his hands, the deep, wounded sound of his interruption flushing back down his gullet into the pit of his stomach.

Emerging from behind the desk to support his friend, Shultz notices the moisture of his shirt. Stephen's chest heaves up and down; after a moment, he regains his composure. Shultz returns to his seat.

"She's not coming back," Stephen sniffles, the skin of his face a sheeted white. "She's gone. I know her. I've known her since she was

19, and I'm telling you, she would never say what she said to me if she didn't mean it."

"What did she say?" Shultz asks.

"She said she didn't love me anymore," Stephen smiles, blinking, the tears and the chuckles he makes morphing into a demented union. "She said she was past me."

"Was there any indication of this happening?" Shultz asks.

"No," Stephen concentrates on his breathing. *No more break-downs. Count to 10. Daddy shot himself in the head, and we aren't going to be like Dad, are we? No? Good. Keep talking.*

"No, we talked about marriage again, and she said what she's said for the past two years, which is she isn't ready. I asked her how I'm supposed to help her, to help both of us, to put us in a position to be happy. She hadn't really let on she was unhappy. She relished in the success we made together, in both of our careers. One of the things she said as she was leaving was how I never paid attention to her needs, and I guess she's right. I've been obsessed with making Bessemer great while promoting my own work."

"Phoebe knew that about you when she agreed to marry you," Shultz shakes his head. "What I don't understand is that everything she's said, she's known. She supported your aspirations, she followed you to Baltimore after your time at UMBC, and she honestly thinks, what, eight years into it that it's a bad idea? 'Sorry, this isn't what I asked for, good luck Steve?'"

"I guess. We've never needed counseling, we never really even fought that much... I can see where she's coming from regarding this past month, though."

"Since when?"

"Since the shooting," Stephen says.

"What does that have to do with this?"

"I don't know," Stephen breaks his eye contact with Shultz.

"Yes you do. I can read you, Christiansen. Don't bullshit me. What happened after the shooting?"

"I started thinking differently."

"You mean like post-traumatic stress?"

"No. Just ... differently. It made me realize how fragile life is, and how lucky I really am, and I guess I don't understand why Phoebe still refused to share in the glory of what we built. If she stood with me during the bad times—and she did—then she should be around when I finally achieve something, right? I'd say the same if she were a friend of mine, but she's so much more than that."

"Where are you getting all of this from?"

"I saved somebody's life—well, not their life, but I ... I intervened, rather—you know," Stephen's explanation peters off.

"No, I don't. What are you talking about?" Shultz asks, completely serious.

"Isaac."

"Isaac?"

"The man who was getting robbed."

"Right. What about him?"

"We've been talking a lot since the incident," Stephen lets out a rickety sigh. "Apparently, he's my biggest fan. He's been through some absolutely awful things in his life. He's only thirty two, four years older, and everything about him has really awakened me."

"You've been through so much too, Stephen."

"No, you don't understand. This man has been through a ringer of events which makes mine pale in comparison. Yes, there's a theory of relativity for grief, but getting to know him made me truly grateful for my own path."

"What does this have to do with Phoebe?" Shultz asks.

"From talking to Isaac, reading his writing, I changed my perspective. I have a great idea for a novel I'm trying to work on, but the whole situation with Phoebe blocked all my creativity and caused me to not be able to write a single word. I sat up thinking about her all the time, how distant she's gotten since the shooting, how much she means to me—all of it, a huge burst of disgusting emotions. I want to show her how valuable she is to me by marrying her."

"Is that why you haven't been sleeping?"

"Yes," Stephen rubs his face. "I keep dreaming that she's drifting away from me. The last time we had a 'moment', if you want to call it that, was on the day I got shot, actually. The morning of, it felt like everything was fine, and that she was perfectly content with what was going on in our lives. After the shooting, my life changed, Charlie. My soul shifted, my passions tilted, I gained a great friend through a horrible situation and I think it made me lose the only thing I've ever truly wanted."

"What?"

"Her."

Silence fills the room.

"Well," Shultz says, playing with a pen on his desk. "You do have to remember that's only your perspective. From what you're telling me, she hasn't exactly been thinking straight either."

"What do you mean?" Stephen wipes his face with a tissue from the box on Shultz's desk.

"You're both adults. You both have needs. If she feels like you're not paying attention to her, or if you aren't valuing her, she might be apt to search for fulfillment elsewhere."

"That makes no sense. I always took her out on dates like we were teenagers, I bought her great gifts, I made it clear that even though I had to be away at times she was the be-all-end-all of what I cared about."

"I understand what your intentions were, my friend, but I do believe she might've felt a tad bit constricted," Shultz explains.

"How so?"

"If you love something so much, it should come genuinely. I understand what you're doing comes from the heart, and I'm not faulting you, but I do believe she interpreted your actions as you compensating for the time you didn't spend with her. You said she started getting more distant when?"

"After the shooting."

"Go further back. This doesn't happen overnight. When did you start noticing a change? When did she start responding differently to the marriage question?"

Slogging through alcohol and rubble, the gears of Stephen's mind turn.

"Two years ago. Maybe a bit longer."

"What happened two years ago? I already know the answer."

"It was the same year *Calls* came out."

"Right, and that's when you evolved and started being taken seriously. Really, that's when you started devoting more time to our pursuits here at Bessemer, if I'm not mistaken," Shultz's chair makes a creaking noise as he pulls the wheels closer to his desk.

"I don't understand."

"She took your devotion to both your third novel and to us as you abandoning her."

"That's stupid. How could—why, for Christ's sakes?"

"I'm not saying it's logical; I'm trying to see it from her perspective. She starts claiming she isn't happy anymore and becomes gradually distant after that point, right?"

"Yeah," Stephen ruffles his hair.

"So, if she feels like you were neglecting her, then she might've found someone else to fulfill her needs."

"What are you saying, Charlie?"

"I'm saying, how sure are you that she stayed faithful?"

"One hundred percent," Stephen responds quickly. *Faithful? Phoebe wouldn't cheat. We were always looking to solve our own problems, not find outside solutions.*

"It's only a possibility," Shultz shrugs. "I don't understand why she'd be so non-committal after a certain point in time."

"That makes both of us," Stephen responds. *Cheating?*

"I'm grieving for you, Stephen. A breakup like this, if you truly think it's over … it takes a part of your soul. It kills me to see you in pain."

"Thanks, Charlie. And thanks for talking to me, it truly means the world," Stephen rises, draping his suit jacket over his shoulder.

"Please keep me updated, and keep trying to edit. I know it's hard, but we need you right now."

"I need you, too," Stephen allows a miniscule grin to escape as he waves from the doorway to Shultz's office.

Shultz watches him go, and then, as he exhales, looks to the picture of he and his own wife. They smile pleasantly.

Arriving to his empty apartment at 5:30 in the evening, Stephen resists the urge to continue to the bar. The rooms seem to have grown larger in the past couple of days, with the hidden volume of his and Phoebe's past creeping to life. He still thinks he can hear her voice from the bedroom, or perhaps catch her face peeking at him from around corners.

Hanging his coat by the door, Stephen walks through the living room and into the kitchen. They'd shared their meals at the small table, big enough to let them relax after long days at work. Stephen turns on a light, and imagines she's sitting at her usual spot in his peripheral vision. As he's been doing since she left two days ago, he turns, half expecting to actually meet her gaze.

In the center of the table sits a small note. Stephen feels his muscles turn to lead as he walks across the kitchen.

Dear Stephen,

Thank you for letting me share your life for the past eight years. You truly shall forever hold a special place in my heart, a place of warmth and love. However, that place is in the past. I am planning on moving back to Pennsylvania in the near future, and I've already collected a good amount of my things while you were at work today. I will never forget when you proposed to me in the field of lights almost eight years ago, and I am unspeakably sorry I could not be the woman you wanted to fulfill that promise I mistakenly made. I wish I could be that 21-year-old girl, but I am not the same person, and I will never be who you want me to be. From the bottom of my heart, I am so, so sorry for that.

I will get no greater joy than seeing you become insanely successful. I am blessed to have been included in your books, and I will treasure the memories we made for as long as I live.

I'm sorry, Stephen. I wish I could love you.

Phoebe Walker

10/19/14

On top of the sheet of paper, next to her signature, glinting under the kitchen lights, sits her engagement ring.

[16]

The East Coast of the United States is home to cities holding millions of different worlds; Boston, New York City, Philadelphia. Baltimore is a port, and sits as a destination point on a group of different highways snaking in all cardinal directions. To travel between Baltimore, Maryland and Philadelphia, Pennsylvania, one must cover nearly 100 miles. Over the nation's history, travelers have taken many different routes to cross that distance. Upon reaching Philadelphia, one can either stay in the city itself or branch out to reach the rural strongholds of America which exist in the expanse between Philadelphia and Pittsburgh.

One way to reach Philadelphia, travelling from Baltimore, is to utilize U.S. Route One.

The window is cold against her temple. When she and her father used to drive this road in her childhood, Phoebe loved to rest her head against the door and drift to sleep. Her Dad always told her to follow her heart, to be confident, bold, and, above all, honest. She doesn't attempt to sleep now. Her arms are folded across her chest, her red coat covering her rosy-pink blouse, her deep blue jeans arching down to her open toed shoes. She hasn't pinned her hair today; she lets it cushion the roughness of the window. Scenery passes by as the journey north continues. It's a Monday night, and not many others traverse the beaten path at the nine o'clock hour; they're all where they're supposed to be. Perhaps she is as well, but sleep will not be tricked by the aching in the pit of her stomach.

"You're quiet tonight," Adam says from the driver's seat. His jacket lies in the back next to two boxes of Phoebe's belongings. An unlit cigarette hangs from his lips. The oncoming smoke mixes with the faint stench of alcohol.

Instead of speaking, Phoebe looks out across the American pastoral.

Adam lights the cigarette and rolls down the window. The back left window opens. Realizing his mistake, Adam holds down a different button. He exhales the smoke with a long breath. Phoebe wrinkles her nose, and sits up straight.

"Do you need to do that in my car?" She asks.

"Sorry," Adam says. He coughs, and then flicks the depleted butt away. Exhaling again, he puts the window up. He turns to look at Phoebe as the road unfolds before them.

"Are you cold?" he asks.

She nods.

"Sorry," Adam says again, turning on the heat. Soon, warm air replaces the cold with a comforting hum.

The fabric of the seat molds to her back the more she relaxes.

"I've been meaning to ask you," Adam turns to look at her again. "Have you ever heard of a band called Brand New?"

"No," Phoebe responds.

"I'm not surprised. They don't put a whole lot of focus on their commercialization." Adam reaches to a side pocket on the door to remove a CD case. On the front, two men in long, dark cloaks, their faces obscured by masks, stand around a corner from a joyous little girl in a pink jacket. Fumbling with the disk, he clicks a button on the console; the radio rises to life. Inserting the disk, he reaches down to the door and picks up a bottle.

"Adam, what is that?"

Stowing the bottle away, Adam asks, "What's what?" He turns to her and smiles.

"The bottle. What are you drinking?"

"Babe, I'm celebrating."

"You're what?"

"Celebrating! I've been waiting for this day for four years."

Wrinkling her nose in disgust, Phoebe sinks back to her side of the car.

"How many have you had?"

"This is only my third."

"In how long?"

"Like an hour, hour and a half."

"Jesus Christ."

"Good song! Glad you mentioned it," Adam clicks the button on the stereo twice. A translucent and haunting guitar plays from the speakers, enveloping and overlapping the smell from Adam's bottle and his cigarettes. Phoebe's heart pounds, but is soon overwritten by a voice drifting from the speakers talking about loneliness and God.

"I don't regularly believe in a God," Adam looks ahead. "But I sure believe in Him today, he gave me the greatest gift I could've asked for," He smiles at Phoebe, who, despite the aching worry of her mind, returns the expression. "I've been thinking about it for so long, I can't believe it actually happened," Adam continues. The road has started to curve slightly, arching gracefully through the open scenery.

"Well, we don't have to think about it anymore," Phoebe places a hand on his shoulder. "I'll be living with my mom as I explain what happened. She'll be stunned for a bit, as I'm sure Grace will be as well, and Dad will shake his head at me. After that, I'll be all yours. They say to wait a month for each year you were together with someone before you start officially dating again, but we don't need to make anything official. Besides, we've already got two years down," She rubs the fabric of his shirt, and she can practically hear the glee enveloping his face.

"You got that right. We don't even need to be secretive about it anymore," Adam chuckles. "I'm waiting for this month's rent to run out, and then I have a buddy who can get me a decent job only a few miles from the sticks. You talk to the hospital yet?"

"I haven't gotten it confirmed, but places are always looking in Bethlehem and Philadelphia. It's within reasonable driving distance. I won't have to worry about it at first, though; my mom will understand," Phoebe says.

"Did you leave anything special for Mr. Wannabee Carver back there?"

"A note," Phoebe turns to peer out the window again. The reflection of the night sky bounces around the car. Raindrops have started to fall, emphasizing the luminosity of the moon.

"I'm sure he'll take that well," Adam says.

"He won't. It'll destroy him." Phoebe says softly. Her hand feels naked.

"It had to happen. This was fate. You can't stop what's meant to be, and if it wasn't meant to be, then it shouldn't happen. You're happy now."

The blips of the green mile markers race by them like phrases being lost in translation, their numbers blurred.

"Right? Phoebe? You're happy now?"

"Yes," she says.

The rain intensifies. The song has now turned into its final lyrical section, where the singer is seemingly asking God to talk to him when he reaches the end.

They pass a sign indicating their lane is going to merge to the left. Adam stays straight, his lips moving to the music. He doesn't put his signal on, and doesn't even consider shifting. Phoebe sees the distance between the shoulder and the road closing.

"Adam?"

"I love you, Phoebe! This is the best night of my life." He reaches down and swigs the bottle.

"Adam, you need to get over," A guardrail glints in the headlights, the rain bouncing off the windshield, the wipers flicking back and forth.

Adam refocuses on the road, and he jerks the wheel to left to attempt to adjust. Over the slick surface of the pavement, the music howling from the speakers in gorgeous beauty, the car's wheels shake and begin to slide.

A car in the lane beside them finds itself with no room to continue, and instead smacks into Phoebe's car on the driver's side door. The car is sent spinning to the median of concrete, physics taking control. As the front of the car in the lane they'd been merging with slams into them, the force of the impact sends Phoebe's head rocketing into the window as the cabin collapses. All seventy five miles per hour they'd been travelling condense into one moment, and her body is crushed on impact while Adam's skeleton compresses between the crunching of the car and the front of the other vehicle, a 2004 Cadillac Escalade; the two are pushed closer together than ever thought possible.

Both vehicles disjoin, the Escalade shooting into a tailspin across the highway until it smacks the center median of U.S. 1, and Phoebe's car's wreckage is finally stopped by the concrete, the engine steaming, the body of the car ruined. The force of the crash killed Adam instantly, especially due to the fact he hadn't been wearing a seatbelt. His brain exploded into a few tiny parts as he was thrown into the windshield.

Phoebe lies against the window for a final time, her happiness, hopes, regrets, and desires seeping out of her. Her last thought, as the night turns to day and her mind engages a final, wonderful swan song, is of Stephen gazing down at her as she lay on his lap, his lips tracing one final, whispered prayer:

"I love you, Phoebe Walker."

PART III

[17]

Pennsylvania's rolling hills do not hold promises today. The sun's rays bounce off reeds which bend in the afternoon wind. In the silhouette of the grassy knoll stands a small, white church. Commercialism does not dare to tread among the back roads and mysteries long solved.

In the middle of the expanse is the Church of St. Luke, where, twenty years ago, a ruby haired girl and her older sister had faithfully fulfilled the covenant between humanity and the Lord. They'd sought refuge from the battles of their early teenage years among the presence of their peers and those from the community who treasured their innocence. The gaze of a young child matures along with the soul, like how a story changes when told throughout the years. The redhead eventually left the congregation when she went to college, straying from her humble roots in order to chase after a fleeting sense of glory which she couldn't find in her homeland. Save for a few visits to see her father or her sister, she forgot about the church which hid in the woods in the time-locked small town. The church never forgot about her. It has waited ten long years to see her again. It has kept its part of the deal as tried and true as God to Abraham, and today is the day it welcomes her home for the final time.

The girl returns in a box of studded silver, with the top closed over her red hair and svelte frame. Her tender gaze rests underneath eyelids never to open for an encore of electric blue. The only unbroken parts of her returned to her home are her memories. At the center of the dais of a crowded room, in front of chairs lining the carpeted rows, sits the casket of radiant platinum. In front stands a huge framed portrait of a gallant and smiling young woman, caught between her teenage years and adulthood in a perpetual winning smile, the same eyes catching the glows from the candles and the overhead beams of the church mixing with the softness of the sun. Beneath the pedestal, similar to the altar in the adjoining church, sits a simple statement:

PHOEBE MICHELLE WALKER
MAY 19th, 1986 - OCTOBER 20th, 2014

In the candles and whispers, Stephen sits in the front row, his stare boring holes in the picture. His suit is as black as his depression, and the whiteness of his shirt betrays the crimson of his agony. In the nine days since she hadn't loved him, and the seven since she'd been found in the remains of her car on the highway with another man, his entire universe has turned itself to rubber. The bottomless depths of the bottles he's bought, the messages of condolence and shock, sound and fury, and eternal questions to which no answers exist all confound his existence. Facing the woman in whom he'd placed his heart, receiving the phone call from the emergency contact forms detailing the scene he'd feared in his nightmares for so long, the beautiful eyes which he'd seen be so happy now only remind him of the pain which consumes him. She'd been the answer, and now all that remains is to ponder.

From the receiving line, a woman in a dress of taciturn black floats to him across the floor, walking quietly between the rows of friends and family. If he looks at her for too long, he sees the living blueprint for the love of his life; she was the first edition of the Walker girls, two years older than her sister, with her dark brown hair not quite as spontaneous. She and her younger sister had been about the same height, with the equally athletic build betraying their differences; for all their physical similarities, each woman's ethos had been unique. Phoebe's loudness and eagerness to laugh was not passed to her from her sister; neither was integrity, or trust. Grace Walker's is the originator of the gaze which Stephen had fallen in love with; the same complexion closed underneath the casket now stares into him, as Grace wraps her arms around his neck. He hugs her back not in strength, but in complacent weakness due to the amount of hugs he's given lately, compounded by the weight of knowing.

They release each other, and Grace offers a tiny, dimpled smile.

"How are you doing?" she asks.

"I'm ok," Stephen can only give the expression of liars.

"No you're not," Grace hugs him again, and he pulls her close. "You're not ok. We're never going to be ok."

All he can do is hold her tightly.

"Not with that attitude," Stephen says softly. Grace offers a laugh, and Stephen winces.

"That's exactly what she'd always tell me, 'not with that attitude, Grace!' *Phoebe, we're not going to be able to get to school on time if you don't hurry up!* 'Not with that attitude, Grace!' Good lord, she knew how to procrastinate."

"I wonder where she learned that from," Stephen looks to the picture, and restrains himself from rushing the dais and punching a hole through the frame. He'd rip off all the heads of the roses he'd bought, he'd destroy the carnations and the buds of death, destroy the vibrant smile. It'd all be ok.

"Certainly not from me," Grace replies. "She must've been so lost, Stephen."

"She was," Stephen mutters. "I don't know what happened."

"It isn't your fault. Couples fight," Grace's voice is a seeping poison.

Muscles in Stephen's face tense in preparation for tears, akin to the smell in the air before rain. Soon, he's hugging her for a third time, his face buried into her shoulder. He wishes he could stand there forever, a monument to his own sadness, soiling the dress of the woman who will never become his sister-in-law.

The gazes from the surrounding audience crawl like spiders upon his back. He can feel her crying too, every broken dream from her childhood leaving her body. Soon, another figure joins the pair. He's a head taller than Stephen, a believer of wisdom instead of shrewd knowledge. The grayness of his hair stands inverted to the youth of his heart, which lies in tatters. Stephen withdraws from Grace, and upon seeing the man, he receives a huge, gruff embrace.

"I'm so sorry, Jim. I'm crying like a bitch at your daughter's funeral."

"I always knew you were a bitch, Stephen, its ok," His expression bleeds the same ache which resonates from Stephen.

Breathing steadily, Stephen takes his seat. Father and daughter join as the receiving line continues to be entertained by a woman in black: Mama Beverly, along with Eddie, Grace's husband. *Stephen, you're a worthless, selfish, miserable excuse for a man.*

The three sit in the front row, hearing Phoebe's favorite music echoing about the parlor. U2 mixes with OneRepublic, with a glimpse of Green Day and Genesis. The lyrics bounce around and attempt to ignite memories from the desert of Stephen's mind, but they find no sparks.

"The last time I saw her, it must've been back in September," Grace shuffles her feet. "We sat around playing all sorts of different music from our childhood. She was such an audiophile back in the day, before all the digital technology screwed everything up."

"I remember those days," Jim responds, wiping his cheeks. "You girls were always so anti-pop. You were more into the rockers."

"Yeah, because she thought Billie Joe was hot," Grace laughs.

"Well, that explains how she chose you, right Steve?" Jim says.

Like a poker player's busted bluff, Stephen smiles.

Back in September was the last time.

"Grace," Stephen allows his chin to rest in the palms of his hand as he continues his staring contest with the portrait. "You said the last time you saw her was in September?"

"Something like that. It's been at least two months," Grace replies, leaning back, her fingers interlaced. "It was before you got shot, I know that much. She hadn't wanted to make the drive as of late, she told me she wanted to be around to take care of you if needed."

The sobbing commences. He feels Grace's arm around his back, and her comforting words coil through the air.

"She loved you so much, Stephen," Grace whispers. "You were everything to her. She always told me about how she couldn't wait to get married, and how you'd eventually raise a family, and how she wanted to make our daddy a grandfather. It was all planned out for you guys."

The embryonic syllables wash away in the rivers which fall into Stephen's hands.

The receiving line begins to fill the chairs around them. A man in a black robe, carrying a Bible, walks to the podium at the front of the room. A great darkness seems to nestle itself underneath the man's vision, his complexion a pool of murky water collected after a storm. His hair is sleek and straight, splaying at the base of his neck, the set line of his face turning upwards to greet certain members of the congregation. He sets the Bible down, placing his hands staunchly on either side of the lectern, and he clears his throat as the murmurs fall to silence.

"Good afternoon. I am Father Lawrence Gruver of St. Luke's Church here in the back woods of Bucks County, Pennsylvania. I am happy to see that all of you successfully navigated your way here today through the swamps and treachery of our roads," A respectful chuckle emerges from the crowd. Father Lawrence takes his glasses out of his pocket.

"We are gathered here today to honor the life of the beautiful Phoebe Michelle Walker. The Walkers have been parishioners of our church since Jim and Bev moved into the area from Philadelphia way back in the 1970's. I became a priest here in '78. It was several years after I started as a clergyman when they brought a young girl with them one day, and then after a couple more years they brought another. She was a little ruby haired, fiery offset to her older sister Grace," He motions to the group sitting at the front of the crowd. Stephen's head is bowed, allowing his ears to grasp every word.

"Over the 18 years Phoebe attended our services, I saw her mature from being a great girl into an outstanding young woman. A lot of us as teenagers find ways to stray from the path, but from the start, Phoebe was different. She was always determined to climb her way out of here, imbued with the spirit which joins us today from the people who formed her. She made a wonderful life for herself in the Baltimore area, but she never forgot where she came from. As many of you know, she found her soul-mate in a writer named Stephen Christiansen, a man of outstanding character, in whom she truly realized her love," Again, father Lawrence gestures to the front row. Stephen feels their attention shift.

"While I knew her from our congregation here at St. Luke's, the people who truly understood Phoebe are undoubtedly more qualified to speak in her remembrance. We'll start with a word from her sister Grace Walker-Carmichael, and we shall join together in prayer as we honor Phoebe's memory. Grace."

Withdrawing a crumpled sheet of paper from the folds of her purse, Grace rises. She walks slowly. Father Lawrence greets her with a quick hug as she reaches the podium, the paper laid out flat in front of her, the microphone buzzing in anticipation.

Unfolding the paper with trembling hands, Grace clears her throat and adjusts the microphone. After a moment, she speaks.

"I was sitting in my living room when I got the news. My younger sister—the loud, funny, and gorgeous girl who owns part of my heart—had been in a car accident. Never in my darkest nightmares had I imagined the young, peppy, hopeful smile of Phoebe ever leaving my life before I left hers. Since our youngest days, it'd been the two of us against the world. I was always the quieter one; she'd be out with friends, and I'd be home enjoying the silence of an open field. She'd come home, and we'd find the magic of the universe hidden in our words; while we'd been opposite sides of the coin, we were sisters of the same soul, simply divided to do God's work in different ways. Whenever I was feeling distressed, or downtrodden, or beguiled, I'd find my sanctuary in my younger sister's spirit. She was smart beyond her years, sassier than she admitted, and could be as stubborn as the wood of this podium, but good Lord, I loved her."

Grace flips the page, her hand shaking.

"People knew Phoebe from the outside in; I had the absolute honor of knowing her from the inside out. When other people saw a confident, career-oriented, unstoppable force of nature, I saw the calmness of the clouds which made up that storm. Phoebe always gave the her best to others, saving her worst for herself. When she had her heart broken in high school, she didn't show it to our classmates; I held her when she cried and she asked me why no man would ever truly want her. I always told her she was perfect as she was, and how she was as much of a guiding light to me as she claimed I was to her. There is no other person who could make me laugh like she could, make me cry like she could, who could claim to have almost killed me by putting too much soap in my bubble bath, who could claim she blamed me for almost setting the house on fire twice trying to play chef in the kitchen, or who could say she inspired me every day by being the only morning person in the house as I wanted to crawl back under my sheets and sleep. She was so excited her freshman year of high school, when I could finally drive her and she didn't have to use the bus anymore, she'd come bounding into my room like she was 10 again and practically tear me out of bed. I scolded her many times for this; she didn't care. She loved me too much. She told me at her graduation from high school that I was her role model. I was the one who blazed her path in the way a celebrity or a parent can't, but only a sister can.

"She was always supposed to surpass me, and I loved watching her fly. I stayed close to home. We drifted. That separation made the time we spent together all the more valuable. She found someone else with whom to cry, to love, and to build a life with. I am so unspeakably proud of her for choosing a man such as Stephen as her partner, for they truly were an amazing couple together. I remember when Phoebe, beaming, brought the, in her words, 'insanely handsome' writer from Baltimore home to this back-asswards—excuse my French, Father Lawrence—country home to meet myself and our parents, and I've never seen her heart grow larger or her smile wider. My own sense of pride absolutely flourished seeing her so happy, and with the care between them ... that kind of love will never die. The little red haired fury I saw through the growing pains of both of our lives, our parents' determination, and our collective joy, grew up to be a nurse who took over the world, one step at a time, with nothing else but those who she loved backing her up as she cut through the fog of the future confidently.

"I know it's the stereotypical thing to say. The older sister is the role model, the one who finds the road, who builds the steps, who clears the forest. Phoebe was, and forever will be, my lighthouse on the distant shore."

The paper crumples beneath her fingers, and Grace's voice shakes. "She stabilized the uncertainty of my life and gave me a direction. Whenever I felt like talking, or felt like reversing a bad day in 30 minutes or less, I'd call her. Her words would ring in my ears for days, turning the malevolence of this world into sense and compassion. Phoebe, I love you so, so, so much. You're my angel, my inspiration, and no matter where I go, you will always be with me.

I'm so sorry I couldn't save you."

Crumbling the paper up, Grace finishes to a round of thundering applause. She walks past those in the front row to fall into the arms of her husband, her sobs echoing through the noise. She sits back in her seat, her face buried. Stephen hears her sniffles as he dissects the portrait on the dais.

He sheds no tears.

He follows the motions of the surrounding people as Father Lawrence re-takes the podium. Father Lawrence references the will of God, and how God is mysterious in his workings. Stephen believes him. He goes on about how Phoebe was as 'honest' and 'true' a girl as he'd ever met. The sentiments are static buzzing around Stephen's head, and he bores through the fabric of the photo as Father Lawrence speaks.

They didn't know. None of these people know.

But Stephen does.

Gazing at him from the dais, Phoebe is 22 for all time.

[18]

He took all of her pictures down and put them in a box. The collection sits beside the couch, pushed next to the coffee table to be used as a footrest. He doesn't have to pretend to do his job anymore; Charlie is letting him take as long as he needs to recover, after he cried into his shoulder and spoke works about how this was unspeakable, terrible, haunting, and tragic.

Stephen's seen tragedy; this is not tragedy.

Tragedy implies that the world can continue after a singular event, to be cut up and contained within certain dates. He can't perform such a dissection like he'd been able to when his father killed himself or his mother passed from cancer. It might be years, decades, or a lifetime before the inflated, bulbous tissues of his broken heart are able to be shoved into a compartment labeled '2014'. Grace took her clothes out of the house via more cardboard boxes; her father took her heirlooms out of his grasp via his own brown box; he can't put the hole in his chest into storage.

Therefore, it must be filled. He must find a way to reclaim the space in his soul, which his body numbs with emotions of shock and disbelief. She'd been [redacted] on him with another man. His brain is a censor. For example, the hole must be filled, so he drinks a lot of alcohol to clot the wounds. There are missing pieces in the narrative his brain won't acknowledge, like how she'll [redacted] be coming home again. She'll eventually come home again, he knows. She'll ask why all the pictures are off the walls, when they'd been a loving couple waiting to get married. His brain's Orwellian disguising of his pain is a simple mechanism, but he won't admit that she's [redacted]. Even her name brings soreness to his lips. The only way to drown such a sensation is to put as much liquid down his throat as possible.

Despite the black boxes littering his mind, the words eventually seep through as ink blotches. She'd been cheating on him with another man for, at Shultz's estimation, two years. That man had been intoxicated behind the wheel of her car, driving stupidly fast in slippery conditions. They'd been travelling north to Pennsylvania; Jim knew she'd been on her way home after the fight. Stephen knows the true reasons for her desire to flee their life in Baltimore. Now, he raises the same poison which indented the sanctity of her death to his own lips, the alcohol cold in his mouth. The television is stuck on a postgame show, spitting out nonsense in voices he doesn't hear. He doesn't feel his bare skin sewing itself into the couch where they'd sat together on so many nights. The quietness of the apartment contaminates the air, and only the ambrosia held in the glass bottle, which makes him wince, shiver, and shake, allows him to continue breathing. His feet rest on the coffee table, with every remnant of the nights they'd spent attempting to answer the essential questions of life buried.

He shall stand no trial. They will never hear the voice which buzzes in his head, as if whispered through a transistor radio:

Why did you kill your fiancée, Stephen? Why couldn't you have been more understanding? You pressured her. You pushed her away. You now drink the same drug which factored into her death, because you aren't enough of a man to face what you did. You weren't able to satisfy her. You were too focused on your own career that you threw away all that mattered; she sought her solace in a regular guy, which you never were. You tucked yourself into a beautiful little oblivion. You now sit as the king to a false empire, bathing in the absence of an autumn night, while a family grieves and your job falls. Do you wonder if she ever thought about you as she fucked him, or if she ever thought about him as she was fucking you? Married couples make love, and you were only in it to justify your own success to yourself after she picked you up from the ground. You used her as a status symbol, which is why you aren't crying right now. Your stunned silence is simply a pre-requisite to a grand collapse.

He raises the glass to his lips, hearing the soft kiss of the drink's swish.

Or, you know, maybe she didn't actually 'fuck' him. Maybe he's the one who she made love to, and when she faked it with you she was waiting for the next opportunity to leave. You're filled with an ego masked by false humility. You aren't even innocent; you're smart enough to know better. Those two thugs, as you called them, who shot you on the street, were forced into their crimes. You had a choice. You chose to live this life, to bury the ones you love in order to make a hill to stand upon. You're the worst kind of man: the willfully ignorant. You knew she didn't want to be asked. You knew she wanted to wait. You knew she wanted to move. You lied to those beautiful eyes to which you claimed to have given your heart; instead, all the motions of love which you saved for yourself were given to her as placebos. Now she's dead, smashed up like a window pane on a highway because she was running from you.

A glass of Jack Daniels holds Stephen on this lonely night. The thoughts bouncing in his mind elicit no reaction. They are a simple droll, a rolling of wind on the side of a house.

Do you think she was really happy as you were happy? How many times do you reckon she faked a smile, faked interest, faked an orgasm to bring you joy? You dedicated all of your books to her as a shoddy compensation. That's the poetic justice—the only justice—which will serve a murderer like you. Most murderers do get to walk nowadays. You're no different. You managed to take all of your privilege, none of which would've been spoiled on a man like Isaac, and throw it away in order to harm the woman you claimed you wanted to marry. You wanted to show the world your success via your puppetry, and now it's your strings which have been severed. God doesn't keep a kingdom in order to placate people like you. The name which you wanted to make by your own hand now is the very element which cuts you free from the graces of fortune, which turns the tides in the middle of this gale now that the lighthouse is gone. You tore it down, and in the process all which you built will be relegated to crumbling ruin in the middle of what would've been magic.

The glass is empty. Stephen walks to the kitchen. Analysis of last weekend's win continues on the television, completely unbothered by his personal immolation. They weren't there to see, in their suits and their legacies, Stephen as he collapsed into Grace's shoulders, or as Jim and Mama Bev buried their brightest joy. The blood on his hands shivers as he pours another glass of golden beige. The hole inside of him doesn't absorb the drink as he chugs it down his throat; it only floats there, the buzz arching through his system, a gastric bypass of emotions. He tosses an empty bottle into the trash, clamoring and clanging. He's been keeping most of the lights off in the house, hiding from the outside. On the calendar they kept on the fridge, he's already marked the day he's going back to work—exactly a week from today, next Monday. He'll boot up his computer later and look at the manuscripts, look at all the errors, that

outpouring of support which is being posted on the same Facebook wall he visited 36 times a couple weeks ago

he's qualified to correct. Shultz will call him a hero for rebounding amidst the fall of his world, the echoes of which shall morph into a vibrant song as he overcomes his demons.

Or.

His hands grip the stainless steel of the sink. Or he won't do any of that. He'll stand here and drink, allowing his throat to become a chute of sadness. People like him aren't supposed to recover from these metric amounts of hurt. He could easily be one of those people. The royalty money will pay for the habits. He doesn't have to foot the funeral costs; that's why they weren't supposed to be married, he figures. God knew. Every prayer he'd ever sent and every word he'd ever written were building to the moment he was shown the truth, when his ribcage burst open and the resilience finally died.

He looks down to his two hands, his arms trembling. He feels his knees begin to bend, mimicking the weakness of their fellow limbs. He doesn't sink. After a few seconds, his stomach looping accordingly, the shaking stops. In the dimness, the soap dispenser burns a reflective orange, plastic bought from the grocery store when she'd been a faithful fiancée instead of a cheating whore. Reaching out his left hand, he pumps the dispenser twice, allowing the soap to caress his palms as a blob. Turning on the faucet, Stephen shifts the handle all the way to the right, the hottest setting. Water gushes out of the spigot. Soon, steam begins to rise from the bottom of the sink, circling the drain. Calmly, Stephen sticks his lathered hands into the stream.

Heat doesn't register on his skin, and he rubs vigorously. His cycle repeats, as he grabs more soap from the dispenser. Once more he sticks his hands back under the water. There should've been a wedding band on one of his fingers, but the absence allows for the water to flow uninhibited. He simply stares at the wall above the sink, flinching as he scrubs his hands even harder. Soon, the skin's color turns to soreness, and he gashes a part of his flesh open with a fingernail. He recognizes the pain, but keeps cleaning. Out of the cut, blood is immediately washed down the drain, the heat of the water intensifying. He collects more soap, and then returns to the scalding water, cutting himself again on the palm, this time in a long line stretching from the base of his fingers to the wrist. The heat surges into the fresh wounds, and now crimson finds its way. The horrors of his deeds flow into the drain out of sight. He must continue to cleanse, for it was he who told her to leave, his palms which pushed her away, his fingers which strangled her hopes and aspirations.

The cuts are not deep, but the warmth fuses itself into the muscles used to write his grand lies. His jagged nail carved a canyon in the skin which once held her face and called her beautiful. Five more times, he scalds himself with the water. No matter how hard he scrubs, the rawness of the skin mixing with the discoloration of the now bloodless cuts, he still knows there's more to wash.

Only one thing will cleanse him.

He smacks the spigot off, and then, with his throbbing left hand, uncorks the lid on the new bottle of Jack Daniels. Taking it in his fingers, he pours the alcohol onto the open cut on his right hand first, and then lathers both hands in the smell of the drink. As soon as the liquid enters the widened gash on his palm, despite his stupor, Stephen cries out. The bottle falls to the floor as he clutches his hand to his chest, his face flushing. Squinting, he slides down the cabinets to the ground, the skin swelling from the burning and the application of his medicine. His sobs echo through the empty apartment where he swears she's waiting around the corners, ready to tell him *I don't love you anymore.*

[19]

The harbor stretches out in front of them in wavy blue. Clinton Street's Marine Terminal houses a collection of iron giants, old ships eking out the rest of their existence. The names of 527 Marylanders are etched in stone on a monument to the Korean War's fallen servicemen. Baltimore's scenery fills the view as Stephen and Isaac sit on the stone foundation guarding a section of trees elevated off the ground. The cobblestones in front of them, a clayish red, stretch ten feet to the water's edge. November's blooming colors carry with them memories on the slight breeze which ruffles their coats, working its way back to the bay. All life returns to the water.

Bandages adorn Stephen's hands like gauzy gloves. Shultz had called him a fool at work today, his first day back, with a sigh and a hint of change in his tone. Stephen's coat, a black North Face, covers his shoulders, his jeans snaking down his folded legs to his sneakers. His body traces the concrete, his hands splayed. He can still type, so all should be well.

All will never be well again.

Coughing, Isaac brings Stephen back to earth.

"Sorry," Stephen shifts on the makeshift bench. "Guess I got caught up in the water."

"I was in the hospital while you were gone," Isaac says.

"What?" Stephen's face is incredulous. "Why?"

"I took too many drugs with the wrong drink. It's the fourth time I've tried," Isaac continues looking out across the water.

Children laugh and slide in paddle-boats, their parents grinning as they follow. Stephen turns away from Isaac.

"It was the night of the 17th, you know," Isaac continues. "The same night you said you were sitting up late attempting to write and drinking your iced tea. I tried calling you, but your phone must've been off."

"I'm so sorry, Isaac. I had no way of knowing. I saw the missed call-"

"I'm not asking you to apologize, Stephen," Isaac turns to him, the easiness of his expression now falling back into place. "I should be the one apologizing to you. It'd been you setting up these lovely conversations between us on your own accord until today. You went back to work, you said?"

"Yeah," Stephen replies, looking down at his bandages.

"I can't pretend to imagine what it's like to have to do that. To return back to your life as if nothing's happened, when the entire world has been ripped out from under you," Isaac says.

"Thanks," Stephen says.

"Don't thank me. You don't have to thank me."

"You're really the only one who I feel like I can talk to about this," Stephen's words are a rush. "Charlie doesn't get it. I'm his employee and his friend. I cut off contact with a lot of people since I graduated college, except for him and her, of course."

"Who is her?"

"Her."

"Who are you talking about? Phoebe?" Isaac asks.

"Yeah." Stephen winces. "Her."

Stephen doesn't meet Isaac's gaze, but he feels it tingling on his cheek like a microscopic insect.

"I've never lost someone like that," Isaac says.

"You've been hurt in so many other ways."

"I don't know what I'd do with myself if I ever lost Olivia. The thought of her leaving completely shatters me."

"I don't know why I'm not shattered, too," Stephen mumbles.

"Hm?"

"I don't know why I'm not shattered, too," Stephen repeats, louder. "I don't know why, but I haven't had a moment where I break down in tears, where everything no longer goes on, where life stops and I no longer breathe."

"You found out she was cheating."

"That shouldn't have anything to do with it."

"But it does." Isaac shimmies down the concrete, and puts his arm around Stephen's shoulders.

"It does," Isaac says again. "You're hurt. There's no roadmap to hurting. There's no blueprint to pain. It works itself on different people in as many different ways, and there's nothing you're supposed to feel or supposed to do to prove it. You're in shock, my brother."

"I know."

Taking his arm off of him, a smile creases Isaac's face as he plays the audience to the roiling families enjoying the day.

"Did I ever tell you about my daughter?" Isaac asks.

"You have a daughter?" Stephen asks, raising his eyebrows.

"Yeah. Well, kind of," Isaac shifts. "She's my sister's daughter. My sister and I only talk once or twice a year now. She's four years older than me, so she has to be what ... 36? I'm older than you, remember, whipper snapper," Isaac chuckles, and Stephen feels something besides a grimace break his face for the first time since Ph- since *she* passed.

"She got with this man who was deep into heroin. He didn't even stick around to see my niece born; he got himself killed in a shooting in Philadelphia. So then it was my sister all alone with this beautiful baby girl named Emma. I always called her Em. My sister caught the addiction of Emma's father like a disease. Soon she was using her welfare checks to buy needles while trying to work a job with a newborn baby at a daycare or at home. One of the people she thought to be a friend tipped off child welfare services and reported the two of them. There weren't any ragged conditions, or anything terrible about the house, just the unseemly gentlemen with whom my sister ... well, whom she got to know. So many people came in and out of that house for all the wrong reasons, and that's who Emma would've seen as her role models if my sister hadn't gotten caught. That pretty much settled the deal. Here's this darling baby girl whose daddy is dead and whose momma is off to jail, and she would've gone to the state, never to be ours again."

Isaac shuffles his feet.

"I was a 22 year old kid. I had dropped out of design school. Didn't have the money to finish it, and fortune simply turned against me. Here was this little pudgy faced angel brought onto this earth into the wrong future. Despite the popular narrative, my parents actually had their lives together fiscally, but they were old and starting to fade. They were in no position to take care of a child. Really, I wasn't either, but I didn't see it as a choice. I told you I used to preach, right?"

"Right," Stephen affirms.

"This was during the same period. I took in this baby girl, my sister's goodness extracted into a package—this is before I met Olivia, mind you—and I attempted to raise her. You truly don't know you've been loved until you love something more than yourself; I don't mean a woman, I mean a little girl who looks up to you and calls you Daddy. Somebody who bases the idea of her life, her view of men, off of your actions. I returned to my parents' house on Charles Street, and I took care of her as much as I could've. I made sure she was enrolled in the right type of schools, made sure she ate correctly, made sure she had a view of the world more stable and less corrupted than the circumstances which brought her into it. We aren't our circumstances, Stephen. We're more than who we've been.

"I raised this girl until she was six. For four years did I bounce from minimum wage jobs; I even finished my degree, believe it or not. Then my sister got out of jail and they gave Emma back. I even met Olivia along the way. Now that little girl who I saw take her first steps, clean up her vomit from the front of her bib, who I taught her first words ... I still talk to her nowadays. She's 12. Her mom got clean. Her mom didn't become part of another statistic, and that little girl still sees me as her father. It's not 'Uncle Isaac' as my nickname; it's 'dad'."

"Wow," Stephen allows the word to rest on his lips. "What happened after that?"

"They kicked me out," Isaac says.

"What?" Stephen asks.

"After Gianna took Em back, there was no reason for me to be there anymore. The money they'd saved eventually ran out. I had to go hungry to put food in Em's mouth when she was there. I had started seeing things, hearing things. The medication was a huge cost, to the point where I couldn't pay my part of the rent. People don't understand, nor do they get trained for, the types of arithmetic I've had to do. Someone can tell you how the two legs of an isosceles triangle are equal in length, but not how to split social security among two senior citizens and a man of 26. They can't tell you how to pay for the expensive drugs you get from the pharmacy or your contribution to the rent. They can't tell you how to cash in a check of love for practical financial use in the world, for as much as Olivia loved me, she wasn't in any better way, and her parents weren't about to let some psychotic trash like me take up their valuable space. I want there to be a calculus course where you have to calculate the limit of a paycheck per month, and then when one gets laid off, how to compensate for that as your toes dip in the snow so you can get the voice of the girl you raised in your head to stop telling you to kill yourself every other night."

The parts of his face Isaac uses to smile are set in a line, a siphon retrieving the past.

"This disease of mine is nasty. It takes the most important things in my life and flips them on me, to the point where I hear Emma, Olivia, talking to me to do it. To finally end the pain which God placed on my shoulders to attempt to bear, only to beat me down again and again and again. That's what happens when the medicine makes you dreary and suicidal to get the voices to stop. The only reason it was four years of experiencing homelessness and not six was due to the fact Olivia and I were both, by the hands of the same Lord for whom I used to be a mouthpiece, able to get jobs and afford the smallest of apartments. He works in mysterious ways, as they say, and He holds an inflection in his heart for the lesser fortunate."

"Isaac ..." Stephen says.

"Yes?"

"How are you ... how are you still standing?"

"I don't want to be, Stephen," Isaac says. "Part of me is saying He's calling me home. My writing describes it as a pull back to the Heaven from whence we all came. The other part tells me to keep fighting, to keep working the factory shifts I am now where the volume of people causes my disease to worsen. Being around crowds when I'm not on the medication causes me to get paranoid."

"Why don't you take the medication?"

"Because part of me doesn't want to die," Isaac chuckles—a humorless, ringing noise. "I'd rather face down a lion at the foot of my bed, claiming to be Satan, after being released at the age of 30 from a mental hospital, telling me about how my faith in God is misplaced, than deal with the dread held in every one of those stupid little blue capsules sometimes. Voices of friends who I don't know anymore call up the stairs to my bedroom at night, or at least they used to, telling me to stop burdening everyone. Sometimes my throat tightens and I start to lose my sight, surrounded by illusions the likes of which you can't imagine until they're staring you straight in the face, saying all the hope is a lie and that Emma would've been better off without having to know a freak like me, that Olivia deserves better. That's why I swallowed the pills and the drink whilst you were away."

The words bounce around Stephen's mouth, amorphous and futile.

"But He's keeping me here for the moment," Isaac says. "He's keeping me here for the smile I see on Olivia's face when I come home, for the glory of that 12 year old girl, for the people with whom I interact and connect with online discussing writing, for the people who know a different type of pain. For you," Isaac touches him on the shoulder.

"I stay alive because you, in the middle of your tumult, are standing here listening to me ramble on like a loser about my past, when *you've* lost your fiancée. Tragedy does not discriminate. It hits you whether you're white, black, Asian, gay, straight, questioning—it hits you if you're human. Friendship isn't about the length of time we've known each other, or the amount of memories we've made; friendship is about compassion, which translates to sharing in each other's pain to keep on living. We join in each other's agony in order for one more laugh to come through, or one more go around after you think you've lost it all. And I have lost it all, Stephen. I've lost it all so many times I don't know how I ever find it again, but I keep going. You've lost it all before. You've told me in passing about your father's death, and now you're staring at this great big black wall which you haven't even acknowledged, trying to be strong to keep your job, trying to be strong to impress me right now. And I'm telling you what Olivia told me: it's ok to not be ok. It's ok to bend, as long as you don't break. I am here for you."

"Thank you so much," Stephen stutters. "I don't know what to say."

"And you call yourself a fuckin' writer?" Isaac laughs, punching him in the arm. "You sure do get lost for words a lot being a man of the page."

"I guess, must be a character flaw of mine."

"That's the college education talking, if I've ever heard it," Isaac chuckles. The two of them see the sun still suspended in the sky, not yet pushed away by the encroaching presence of winter. For a Monday, the amount of families basking in the glow of Baltimore's uniqueness breathes auspiciousness.

"I have a … hypothesis," Isaac says, after a few seconds of silence.

"What's that?" Stephen asks.

"I am allowed to say this as a black, fiscally disenfranchised, schizophrenic—mentally ill—man living in America today, alright?"

"Alright."

"Hippies," Isaac says.

"What?"

"The hippies were right."

"Ok."

"Man, I know I told you before, but people have been walking past me my entire life. When I was homeless, I could've sworn I was as invisible as one of these damn trees around this park," Isaac gestures to a maple tree sitting across the sidewalk, eavesdropping, catching pieces of their conversation on the afternoon wind.

"People walk by these trees and they don't ever appreciate them, you know? Remember what I was telling you a minute ago in my rant?"

"It wasn't a rant," Stephen says.

"Play along. What did I say?"

"You said a lot."

"Holy shit, you're dense for being an author," Isaac chuckles.

"Hey. That hurts my feelings."

"Good. I said how people need to bend and not break, right?"

"Right."

"Well, that's what trees do. So many people have been where I've been, nestled on benches and hidden underneath canopies of these very limbs. Some have almost snapped. I've been found standing after the roughest winds imaginable time and time again for whatever reason. All of these trees, all of the people who you see in low places— they're all human beings. If people actually took the time to listen to them, they'd understand the majesty in what they ignore, and how an everyday object like a maple or an oak holds one of the biggest secrets to everyday life."

"That's really deep, man," Stephen says. "You should be a poet. The classical Pre-Socratic philosophers would applaud the application of those ideas."

"You think? You think that's worth writing down?"

"Absolutely. People really don't pay attention enough to those kinds of nuances."

"Fine," Isaac says, standing, stretching his arms. "I know what I'll do. I'll imbue myself with the inspiration from my author friend, the great Stephen Christiansen of Baltimore, and I'll write a book. One day, I'm going to finally write a book more complete than the scraps I pieced together for that manuscript you so graciously read."

Standing in front of Stephen, Isaac beams, an almost boyish look to him.

"You know what I'm gonna call it?" Isaac asks.

"What?"

"*The Theory of Talking to Trees*. Eh? How's that for a title, author boy?"

Standing with him, Stephen follows him down the sidewalk.

"I like it. I really like it," Stephen says.

"Do you?" Isaac presses as he waits for Stephen, to walk beside him down the path. "Don't you be lying to me. If it sucks, tell me it sucks. I've dealt with a lot worse, my pride can take it."

Soon, their voices are covered by the passing cars and the echoes of their shared souls, fading as the sun aims to dip below the horizon.

[20]

Pens in the holder rattle like bones as Shultz's fist meets the top of his desk; a moment later, he's storming down the hall.

"Stephen!" He yells. He approaches the open door to Stephen's office. Stephen looks up from his laptop, which hums next to a drink.

"Stephen, what—is that a bottle of Jack?" Shultz is befuddled, clutching wrinkled papers in his hand.

Looking at the bottle momentarily, like it's a stranger, Stephen tells Shultz, "Yes. It's my first today, actually."

"Today? Listen, I know it's your second day back, but you can't be drinking on the job."

"Why not?" Stephen asks, fidgeting with the cap.

"Because, this isn't college. And that reminds me—what is this? What did you send me?"

"The finalized edits on *Her Favorite Paralegal Vampire*." Stephen smirks.

"Cut the shit, Stephen. These aren't the edits. This is ... I don't know what this is," Shultz flips through the pages quickly. "It isn't what you think."

"What do you mean?" Stephen cocks his head. "I sent you the finalized version of Blaine Krinkle's manuscript you told me to finish."

"Really?" Shultz quips. "Did Blaine Krinkle know Phoebe too?"

"The hell are you talking about?"

"You sent me a document called 'Random', and when I opened it I read such gems as: *her auburn blonde hair weaved through my fingers. I'll never feel it again, I don't even deserve the memory. I killed her, I-*"

"Shit," Stephen is up out of his seat in a flash, walking over to Shultz and attempting to snatch the papers from his hand. Shultz lets them drop, growling in disgust as he slams the door to Stephen's office shut.

"I'm sorry, Charlie. I must've sent the wrong document."

"Yeah, you can say that again. I only read the first paragraph and I could tell it was the way you're coping with all of this."

"It's my next project," Stephen says. Shultz waits for an indication that what he's heard is a punchline; he doesn't get one.

"You can't be serious."

Anger primes Stephen's voice, and he snaps, "What? It's what I've been working on. It's the novel, the follow up to *Calls to a Crowded Room.*"

"Steve," Shultz plants his hand on Stephen's desk. "You can't do that. You *cannot* write a parable about your fiancée for your next release, it would be career suicide."

"According to who?" Stephen asks. "According to you? Really? You're going to tell me what to write now?"

"Listen, I'm being extremely lenient. I can tell you're hurting, and-"

"Don't you placate me. I know exactly what you think."

"Oh, do you?" Shultz responds. Stephen places the papers back in their proper order as he stands near the window. "Please tell me what I think then, Mr. Christiansen."

"I think you're losing money because of me and you don't want to fire me because I'm your friend."

"Well, holy hell, someone's a mind reader!" Shultz shrugs.

"I've drug myself through so much mud for you, and this is how you're going to repay me?" Stephen says, walking over to his desk to pick up the Jack. He stows it in the chest pocket of his suit jacket.

"Excuse me?" Shultz is quickly incredulous. "*You* got drug through the mud for *me?* Are you kidding me?"

"No. I'm not stupid, Shultz. I'm your biggest sale. My three novels are your top revenue generators across the entire United States. I mean what the hell, did you really expect me to pump out something like Delfino's *Bloodbath Sunrise* or the other shit we choose to accept?"

"You might be all that you described, but I refuse to publish whatever it is you're working on if it's going to be a thinly veiled attempt to justify your feelings in regards to your fiancée's death."

"Justify? I'm not justifying anything," Stephen's fingers quickly find the bottle in his pocket. Before Shultz can say a word, he pops the cap off. It skitters on the carpeted floor, and he takes a large swig. Panting, he continues. "I'm not justifying shit. I know I killed her."

The tenacity of Shultz's voice deflates. "Steve-"

"No, you're right. I killed my fiancée. It's almost like I threw her into the path of that car by pushing her away to the other man."

"You didn't do anything like that, and you know it. Is that what you really think?"

"I don't think it," Stephen wobbles as he bends over to collect the fallen cap. "I'm basically writing a fictionalized confession. I know exactly what I did, it's not a possibility."

"Are you in therapy right now?"

"Sort of," Stephen responds. "The one friend who I talk to about this has tried to kill himself four times because his life is infinitely shittier than mine, and the other is my boss. How fucked am I?"

"You should really be seeing someone, Stephen. Usually they say to wait until you're able to talk about it, but in your case, this is deeply starting to impact your work."

Stephen's head jitters with every word Shultz says like a radio antenna atop a car.

"My entire Platonic existence has always impacted my work," Stephen says. "That's been my life. The plots to all my novels have drawn from real shit. This is how I articulate and share my pain. Either that, or I'd have jumped off a high bridge and gone splat a while ago."

"Are you sure that's your first bottle of the day?" Shultz asks. "You're way too philosophical for 9 AM."

"Don't you remember? I had Philosophy back in college at this time, it's no big deal," Stephen wanders over back to his seat and sits down. "Now, sir, if you'll excuse me, I'm going back to editing."

"I thought you said you managed to get the edits for Krinkle's manuscript finalized."

"See," Stephen holds up his hands in front of him, as if telling Shultz to stop. "I could've, but these bandages on my hands are really annoying."

"How did ... did you cut yourself again?"

"No, no, no, I had that accident washing my hands the other night. You know, the one you yelled at me for my first day back."

"That accident now involves added gauze and medical wrap? Did you lose a fight with a block of cheese and high-five the knife?"

"No, like I said, it was an accident. But it's messed up my motor control, so I can't hunch over my computer like usual," Stephen puts his entire chest on top of the laptop.

"We're going to have an issue. We can't delay production on these manuscripts. Our publication runs --"

"On a fine schedule. Yes, Mr. Shultz, Director, Commander, Commandant Shultzy my darling, I'm aware," Stephen rubs his temples. *How many bottles has it been?*

"I think I know what needs to happen here," Shultz says.

"What's that?" Stephen leans back, putting his feet up on the desk.

"I think you need more time off."

"Do I?" Stephen grins.

In an instant, he rushes to stand in front of Shultz.

"Is that what I need, Charles?" Stephen yells. He walks to his desk, and tosses a stack of papers onto the floor, fluttering like bodies of dead birds.

"Is that what I *need*? Do I *need* to go back home and see my fiancée all around my house when she isn't there, to imagine how long she'd been cheating on me with that mother *fucker* Adam?" Spittle flies from Stephen's lips, falling to rest on Shultz's shirt. "Do I *need* therapy? Does this company no longer *need* me, am I fucking not *needed* now that you've thrown my creativity under the bus like I'm a fucking object?" Stephen slams the stapler on his desk repeatedly with each word.

"For your money?" Stephen tosses the stapler to the floor, where it cracks in half. Jabbing a finger into his own chest, he screams, "I built this goddamn place up from the ground with you, this was *our* dream together, one that isn't currently lying six fucking feet under the earth with the dried blood of a worthless piece of alcoholic shit splattering what remains of her fucking *head*, you asshole!" Stephen's fist rockets down on the desk, nearly missing his computer. He walks back up to Shultz, slapping his dress pants with his bandaged hands.

"You think this is my fault?" Stephen asks.

"I never said it was your fault," Shultz whispers.

"That's what you're implying. I don't need any more time off."

"You're including errors in the manuscripts you send to be published."

"Maybe I'm tired of correcting mistakes," In the same flash it took him to ignite his rage, Stephen tries to sit back down in his chair, but misses. He falls to the floor, and instead rests on the ground with his elbows on top of his knees. Panting, he glares up at Shultz, his irises burning.

"If you weren't my roommate, and the co-founder of this company, I would fire you right now," Shultz tells him. He's remained perfectly still.

"How about you do what I already know you want to do. You stopped seeing me as your friend when I became tied to this company's money."

"Believe what you want," Shultz shrugs. "It's your opinion, Stephen. Whatever will make you feel better, I'm letting you say. I'm counting to ten and not Sparta-kicking you through the window behind you right now. If that's me not being a friend, then, well, ok."

Shultz removes his phone from his pocket, and checks the time.

"I have a meeting in fifteen minutes. You have one of two options. One, either get back to the standard of the excellent work you're known for, or, alternatively, take the next week off, go home, get rest, get help, and stop doing this to yourself."

A rattled, insane laugh from Stephen fills the room.

"You got it, boss. You got it. I guess I'll see you in a week."

He stands up, pulling himself back to his feet via the desk. Snatching his coat from the back of the chair, he throws it over his shoulders. He disconnects his laptop, shoving it into his bag and zipping it. Throwing it over his arm, he takes the bottle of Jack out of his suit coat's pocket, now tucked comfortably under his north face, pops the cap, and takes a large swig. Finishing, he licks his lips at Shultz.

"When did you start doing that?" Shultz's brow furrows. "You never did that in college."

"I was also dating her back in college."

"Who?"

"You know who. My therapeutic centerpiece, according to you."

"We were different men back in college," Shultz says.

"Exactly. That's exactly what I am now. I'm a different man, a much, much different man."

"I'm here if you need me," Shultz shrugs.

"Fuck you."

"No thanks."

"Seriously, Charlie, fuck you. You say that, and you don't know. You're a privileged, entitled, father riding sack of shit who has a wife, has a great job, and who doesn't understand the value in having to struggle. I don't mean sit back at your desk and dictate to people who you look down on, I mean actually work, I mean work with your *hands*," Stephen flexes, his fingers coiling like insects. He drops the Jack to the floor, where it spills out burgundy-gold colored blood.

"You're a cocksucker. I really don't know why it took me this long to see that."

"I think it took your wife—sorry, *fiancée*—banging another man," Shultz bites.

"Yeah, you know, it probably did."

"The pot calls the kettle black, and the great author throws stones in houses made of glass to see if he's actually able to break anything worse than he broke himself. Are you done? You're grieving, but I don't have to take your bullshit," Shultz says.

"You ever read the Bible, Charlie? I know you didn't back in college," Stephen bends down to pick up the fallen bottle.

"Not recently."

"My friend Isaac used to be a preacher," Stephen says. "And as Proverbs, chapter 16, verse 18 so eloquently states: 'Pride goes before destruction, a haughty spirit before a fall.'"

"Look at how you've fallen," Shultz smirks.

Breathing fast through his nose, Stephen shakes with rage. He pushes past Shultz, heading out the door. Shultz's smirk falls to a frown as he hears Stephen leave. He only lives around ten minutes away, so he should be able to drive without too much incident. Shultz can only look at the stained floor, letting the murmur escape his lips.

"Do we even have a janitor?"

[21]

Neighbors don't visit Stephen's apartment. They hadn't visited Stephen and Phoebe when both had been tenants, and Stephen doesn't expect anything to change. With Phoebe's items gone, the voices from the streets outside now drift to him through the walls as the only stymie to his isolation. He lies in their bed and imagines the way in which, when they'd been in love, they'd basked in the peacefulness of the night. They'd been locked in adoration, absorbed by passion, and their tongues had spoken the words of infinity.

Despite his fame, he'd never been a quintessential, clichéd high school football star, standing underneath the lights of the stadium with a beautiful cheerleader in his arms. When he'd been with her in this bed, the low glare of the room illuminating only their outlines, all their flaws shared without shame and seen as, instead, beautiful accidents, he'd felt lucky. His entire mission throughout their relationship, when he'd brought her roses to ask her out on Valentine's Day back in their Sophomore year at UMBC, when they'd been worried about a potential child after a condom breaking, to the morning on the day he'd gotten shot, was to ensure she'd never felt used. Lying amidst the cold, the next bottle of alcohol adorning the nightstand—along with a bucket on the floor—the covers do not warm him. Instead, his skin feels the absence of another body touching his, a head to be placed in the crook of his shoulder, a heart to beat against his chest; hair to play with, a soul in which to pour his vulnerabilities, a voice whispering words more important than anything in the world.

For what could be the fiftieth time, he rolls over; the wrinkles of the bed lie undiscovered; the mattress now belongs to him. He used to be shielded from the glare of the red alarm clock, the numbers displaying the date and time of 12:18 AM on November 11th, 2014. To him, the temporality means nothing, for all the hours and all the days are now convalescing into an amorphous blob. His headaches are now constant, a steadfast anchor in the boiling water of his life. He no longer dreams, and the memories, now reminders of a sacred time, are not recalled in joy.

Tossing the covers away, he rises. His tank top sticks to his shoulders. His gray sweatpants do not deflect the breeze which seems to constantly shift through the house. He doesn't foresee his glibness returning to him, nor a sense of aspiration. The steps he treads on his way to the living room are soft, before he remembers there's nobody to disturb.

Plodding over to the couch, he turns on the light and then rests his body on the left hand cushion. His foot taps the box which sits underneath the coffee table, hidden but still lingering in view. Before he can stop himself, he bends down, pulls the cardboard into his lap, and feels himself prying at the box's lid.

Despite the digital age, she'd always been one to print out the best pictures to adorn the walls. The photos are laminated, their plasticity tapping against his fingers; he's careful not to smudge the faces. The frames have been discarded, taken away with the morning trash a week ago. The preserved fossils are now his to revere, and the first already causes his blood pressure to rise and his creeping emotions to stir.

It was a blustery day at Wildwood, a boardwalk in New Jersey. Games galore, different thrift stores, and merchants hawking wares lined the commercialist, yet strangely authentic, rows which overlooked the glory of the ocean. From the way they're standing, with the beach silhouetted behind them, they're probably looking at a few of those shops. *A trinket salesman? An arcade?* Stephen scratches his hair. *This'd been when?* Flipping the photo over, he checks the date. August 4th, 2010. Four years ago, so they'd been either 24 or 25. Well, he could calculate the date—if he just remembered what the little plaque on *the* picture had said at the funeral.

Who took this picture? It isn't a selfie. He's got his hand around her waist. She's wearing sandals, the rest of her legs exposed, running up to the bottom of her bikini obscured by the falling hems of a green shawl, which wraps around her chest to keep her torso warm. He's actually shirtless, for once, with his hair still wet from the ocean, spiked and disheveled from the salted waves, his right hand clutching a bag of their stuff. Her face is partially obscured by sunglasses, and her hair imitates its usual carefree coil while suppressed by a homely beach hat. Both are smiling, not *pretending.*

Placing the photo aside, Stephen continues the tangible slideshow. Next in the series is her college graduation picture. A pang in his chest reminds him how she's the most gorgeous woman he's ever seen. She'd worn a shiny red sash around her shoulders, adorning her black robes. His own graduation photo still hangs in the bedroom; they'd been situated next to each other. Good lord, he could honestly talk to her face all day and never grow tired, never grow fatigued from the energy in *those eyes.* He'd almost forgotten how pretty they are. He'd seen them in darkness, in sunlight, in the reflecting beams of a car as it slammed into the median of a road with a guy named A-D-A-M driving and

Quickly, he places the graduation photo down, and his heart stops. The third photo in line was the one which was hidden the quickest, but somehow it's worked its way to the front of the group.

He'd cried that night. He can still see the tears on his cheeks, and her cheeks, in the illumination from the Christmas trees. Winter hangs in the trophy of the lens; while snow doesn't fall, the air is alive from the heat of the moment reacting with the December cold. A scarf wraps around her neck, her black coat doing its best to warm the body of the 21 year old girl as she clings to the arm of the 21 year old man. He'd stayed in shape since then, but his face used to be so much younger, without the untamed scruff. His entire body wracks with chills, the same he'd felt on that night. A passerby had taken the photo at their request. With his arm around her, she's holding up her left hand so the camera can see the piece of jewelry which now sits at the bottom of this very box. The Christmas lights which permeate the field in the background of the photo, behind the small red bridge on which they stand, seem to congregate like worshippers to a church. Her smile breaks through the tears of happiness which stain both their faces. In one photo lies the life taken from them.

Phoebe Walker had been supposed to die as Phoebe Christiansen.

That's who she is. Phoebe. That's *her*. The name breaks through the walls of the pronoun he's been replacing her name with since he lost the ability to scream and feel the pain which now rockets from the depths of his mind into every fiber of his body.

He drops the box, the pictures bouncing as they hit the floor. The engagement photo now lies on top, and Stephen stands. He grabs a stack of magazines from the coffee table and tosses them headlong at the ceiling, and they crash back down like airplane wreckage. He grabs the lamp, which used to be used as light for the room, and spears it at the television set. Its base punctures the LCD screen, and soon protrudes headlong through the frame. He flips the coffee table, sending all its materials tumbling. Grabbing the table by its legs, he chucks it at the wall. It splinters and cracks, bouncing across the carpeted floor. Jumping, he hits the couch and sends it sprawling into the path near the apartment door. The cushions are ripped off, and he proceeds to the kitchen, unable to hear anything but her name.

He knows not to touch the fridge, for if it falls on him he may be trapped and die. But who cares? Who cares now that Phoebe Walker is gone, and Phoebe Christiansen shall never *be*? The table at which the couple used to eat is upended, the four surrounding chairs thrown aside. Walking over to the pantry, he takes the plates out of the cabinets and smashes them one by one—the oblong discuses break easily. He snaps one over his knee, and doesn't even bother to feel the sting. Destroying the glasses comes next, and he chucks them at the wall like a pitcher. Jagged pieces of the plates and glass litter the ground like corpses; Stephen's bare feet push through them unquestioning, his ears still ringing. Making his way back into the living room, he spies the box of photos on the floor again.

Taking a knife from the fallen silverware on the floor, he walks towards the box, but then remembers the bedroom. He walks quickly, heading for the pillows. With a deft stab, he nails the one which used to rest her head. He picks it up like a wounded animal and walks back out into the living room. Wrenching the couch back up from its fallen position, he sits on the wood which supported the cushions. The knife is tossed to the side, and his hands now rip through the pillow's guts, covering him in feathery static as he imagines each and every time she lay with him. At some point, he realizes, he started bawling like the bitch he is, and now his limbs hurt as there is no more to tear, nothing more to break, nothing more to even bend. She's gone, she's gone, she's gone. *Phoebe.* He hugs the decimated pillow to his chest, sobbing.

A knock comes from the apartment door.

[22]

"You're terrible at this texting thing," Isaac laughs, the night reflecting around him. Stephen's hair stands on end, the door wide open, matching the shape of his mouth.

"Isaac ... what are you doing here?"

"You called for me," Isaac says. He's wearing a different jacket tonight, one of a cool blackness as if he's donning part of the sky. His typical jeans shimmer in the beams from the lamps of the apartment complex. Stephen looks down to his own sweat-stained, feather-laden shirt and sweatpants.

"You could've given me some warning, you know. I would've at least cleaned up after myself," Stephen pants.

"I saw all the warnings, my friend. I saw them in the ways you were talking, in the way you reached out to me when I've been low recently. As God told you to intervene in my situation on the street, I come to you now to return the favor."

Shuffling his feet, Isaac waits for the invitation.

"Uhm."

"That was poetic," Stephen says.

"Thanks. Can I come in?"

Stepping back, Stephen shows Isaac in, and the door drifts shut behind them.

◇

"Jesus, man," Isaac stops in the middle of the living room, surveying the wreckage. The two sit only a few feet apart on the couch, replete of cushions, with Stephen's fingers absently twirling loose pillow feathers. The knife which he'd used now sits discarded near the scattered pictures on the coffee table. The deluge was a rash of his agony, and it tore the elements of the home into shreds. Two survivors now remain in the aftermath, and a haunted expression crosses Stephen's face.

"I guess this is what it looks like," he says.

"What, this? What is this supposed to look like?"

"It's like one of those relief shows you see on television after a natural disaster, and now I guess that's the point. I've broken all these things which reminded me of how good life was before, and it made me stab into the pieces of the universe which contained the last shreds of what I knew," Stephen shrugs. "It's cosmic."

"I don't know if I'd chock this one up to the cosmos," Isaac picks up a handful of the pictures, gently untouched by the maelstrom. "Wow," Isaac whispers. "She was beautiful."

Resting his elbows on his sweatpants, Stephen nods.

"Yes she was. I almost forgot."

"You didn't forget." Isaac flips through the photos, turning them over to view the dates.

"But I want to."

"No you don't, you *think* you do."

"No, I really do. I want nothing more than to tie myself to the rudder of a boat in the middle of the harbor and let it take me out to sea," Stephen says.

"I haven't thought about that one yet."

"I'm sorry. I shouldn't be talking like this around you."

"Why?" Isaac looks up. "Why shouldn't you talk about it around me? We're feeling exactly the same, Stephen. Why would you go silent now, in the moment when you need to be heard the most?"

"It's not supposed to be that way for me," Stephen's voice strains. "I'm not supposed to need the help. I'm not supposed to be the one who calls people in the middle of the night."

"You texted me, you didn't call."

"I don't even remember texting you."

"You did. I know you did. You know you did. It was before you started ripping all this shit apart like some deranged gorilla," Isaac opens his phone and shows him a text message, time-stamped 12:15 AM, November 11th, 2014.

"Ok, fine, I guess I did. But I truly don't remember that happening."

"What do you remember, then?" Isaac shuts his phone and puts it into his pocket. "It isn't the silence you're talking about. It isn't the desire to be quiet when the world needs to hear your words ringing out like a song, now is it? You don't remember silence; nobody ever does, until the noise is so loud you forget what it's like."

"I remember a field," Stephen says.

"A field?"

"A field."

"What was in the field?"

"Lights."

"Ok."

"The most beautiful lights you can possibly imagine," Stephen recounts in awe. "It was December 21st, 2006. It was an absolutely gorgeous prelude to winter, when the snow was hanging in the clouds, waiting to cover the ground in the middle of a small Pennsylvania town she'd wanted to show me."

"Who is she?" Isaac asks.

"Her."

"Who? You need to tell me who."

He finds the words buried under the monuments in his head.

"Phoebe."

"Yes, Phoebe. Say her name. She deserves to have her name spoken."

"Does she?" Stephen asks, pounding his fist into his palm. "Does she deserve to have it spoken after cheating on me for the past two years?"

"Yes," Isaac responds. "She does."

"Why? Why does she deserve that?"

"It isn't a question of what we deserve, Stephen. Life happens to everyone and it doesn't care if you've been the best mother a kid could ask for, you still can get cancer. It doesn't matter if you killed two people and managed to avoid a death sentence, you could live to be eighty. The Lord could be just as apt to send you to heaven or root you in hell for being a homeless black man on the streets who wanted to take care of his niece, we are not the ones to judge His actions, and we are not the ones who make the final calls on who is worth remembering. We are supposed to be different; it's our responsibility. This world is a mix up of people who look to cast judgment; I don't hold hatred for those who spat on me when I was down, or who mock me today. I can only judge myself, and base my actions on being better than who I was yesterday."

"Great," Stephen says. "Great. So now I'm supposed to let the feelings go?"

"No. You remember them. You work through them. You give them the breath of life and the birth of wings to be handled in a way which will save you. Now, keep telling me about why you keep going back to this field."

"It was the moment I proposed to her," Stephen stands up. "It was the moment everything was going to be ok."

"What was going to be ok?"

Rising and falling quickly, the muscles of Stephen's chest constrict as they had at his mother's funeral, his father's funeral, at the news of Phoebe's crash.

"My dad committing suicide, my mom dying from cancer, every

time I looked into the darkness and was calmed by her peace."

"She couldn't fix those things for you. Only you can."

"But she *could've!*" Stephen exclaims, his voice rising. "She could've! We would've been an outstanding husband and wife."

"You already were, you didn't need a title."

Stephen slowly sits back down on the collapsed couch.

"Let me tell you something," Isaac shifts, leaning in to Stephen. "I was broken at a point in my life. I'm still broken now, as you know. I'm bending and swaying every day, worried that I'm going to snap and toss myself over the edge into oblivion where I belong, to go home to God like I've been called to do. I may still go."

"Don't say that," Stephen interjects.

Putting his hands up, Isaac says, "This isn't about me, though. I'm talking about a girl who saw me as more than material possessions, who stuck with me through the disease which corrupts my mind and taints my courage." He hesitates, and then radiates as he says her name. "Olivia."

"No."

The word halts Isaac mid-sentence, the air waiting in his lungs, but Stephen rips the breath from his throat and freezes his blood.

"You're going to tell me how she saved you, right?" Stephen asks.

In the low light of the room, Isaac swallows.

"You're going to tell me how this woman of yours brought you out of the darkness," Stephen's voice is low. "How she taught you to love again after you'd been so beaten, built you when you'd been so ruined, how it took someone to hurt you to know you cared for them after all." Stephen nods his head, his shoulders pale in the moonlight.

"I don't know how the two of you met," Stephen raises his voice slightly. "I don't know your world, but I know the universe; I don't know your fiancée, but I used to know someone like her. You might mention how she pulled you out of the depths of your mental illness, how it was her hands which smoothed over the scars and sewed shut the linings of your soul so ripped due to the cruelty of this life.

It was her shine that broke through the blackness with compassion, her faith which trumped your doubt. Against all odds, when you'd picked yourself up off the floor, she was the one who stood there and whispered 'keep going' when your own head was ready to scream, and crack, and break instead of bend so all which was wrong with the world would be laid bare, and she wouldn't care."

Breathing, Stephen dilutes the density of his words with a quick laugh.

"You'll detail an amazing story about the power of love. You'll speak of the nights you tried to hurt yourself—when you *did* hurt yourself, but God sent you back to us for a reason. God sent you back to *her* for a reason. You'll say there's no other feeling in the world like when you give yourself to someone else, and how your own worth is lifted to a higher level of adoration by the soul of a simple woman who meant *everything*."

Kicking aside the debris, Stephen kneels down in front of Isaac. The hurt between the two of them is a bridge, and their baited breaths are the water.

"I could not be happier that you found and have kept a love like yours, Isaac," Stephen's face is genuine, his voice enveloping and soft. "I used to have a love like that. That's what I stood upon when my own foundations cracked, what I laid upon when I landed on my back, what I grasped when I was falling down and what gave me air when I thought I'd choke. I used to walk upon that shore, but now I'm nothing but adrift; I would give anything to go back to find all which I thought I had, but I know in my soul that she's gone. That person I loved is gone, and now I'm left to face the fact that she might not have been that person at all."

"Stephen," Isaac's voice is small. "I can't even imagine."

"I wouldn't wish this reality on anybody, my dear friend. But it's my reality. And I have a choice to make," Stephen straightens. He returns to his place beside Isaac on the couch, the bare frame rough on his bones. "We all have a choice to make. We're constantly told how the world is full of nice people, and I think it was Bill Murray who said if we can't find one, we have to be one. Could you imagine that? Isn't that ironic? I'm sitting here talking to a suicidal schizophrenic and I'm quoting a comedian. But you know why that is, Isaac? You know why this narcissistic, gullible, ignorant author quotes comedy at a time like this? Because that's the only thing I can do. I would have every excuse in the world right now to sit here and say I'm defeated. I'm lost. The woman to whom my heart belonged is gone, I'm failing at my job, I'm drinking, I'm covering my wounds with alcohol to see if I can still *feel* it," Stephen picks up a bottle from the floor and pours the contents over his barely-mended hands. Isaac watches him from the safety of the other side of the couch. Stephen lets the bottle fall.

"I feel it. And it hurts like nothing I've ever comprehended, how every kiss I was given for the past two years since she started cheating might as well have been a lie, how every time I said goodbye to her she was leaving for another man. But Isaac," Stephen says. "Why do we continue on? Why after your four attempts at suicide have you been sent back here?"

"I don't know," Isaac says. "I don't know."

"But we're here," Stephen affirms.

"We're here," Isaac mimics him, the words swirling on his tongue.

"And we have an option. We grieve. We hurt. We fall down and we get completely desecrated by all we thought holy; betrayed, violently kicked around with our resolve broken and our spirits shattered. This world can take everything from us except one thing. One slice of this earth is dependent on us and those we care about, and no matter how many of my bones get broken or my stars get stolen, how many of those bullets hit me or if I'm knocked down to the point of no return, they cannot take one possession of ours from us as long as we have ourselves and somebody to depend on," Stephen's soaked hand clasps the shoulder of Isaac's coat.

"Hope," Stephen's voice cuts through the heavy air. "That's the gift you've given me."

From the window, an onlooker would simply observe two men embracing each other awkwardly, perhaps a sly joke of a sexual nature waiting on their forked tongue. They'd see them hugging in the middle of a destroyed apartment, with bottles of alcohol and iced tea scattered everywhere, old pictures strewn about, and each letting their emotions flow in a way some might see as a sign of weakness. For those who have been so unfortunate not to have been touched by the gift shared between Isaac and Stephen on this night, it may seem strange to them.

They don't understand that kind of strength.

PART IV

[23]

November 20th, 2014

As usual, Shultz knocks before entering. Stephen stops typing with a jolt, his newly acquired reading glasses twitching slightly.

"Good morning, Director Shultz," Stephen says, taking off the glasses to clean them with the napkin on his desk.

"Good morning, Mr. Christiansen," Shultz looks around at the open carpet, the soft classic rock music playing from the laptop, the ear-buds dangling free on the desk. Stephen sits with his hands in his lap. Shultz's inspection flits from Stephen to the laptop and back again, his eyebrows arcing.

"We sure are hard at work, aren't we?"

"Yes, sir," Stephen says, his posture perfect.

"I am extremely pleased to say I found no errors upon reviewing the last three manuscripts you've edited. It seems as though you've worked your way through the woods back to the beaten path."

"Thank you."

"You're welcome. When the hell did you start listening to U2 again?" Shultz lifts the black buds to dangle near his ear.

"I don't know, I guess it must be a taste Phoebe gave me," Stephen flinches slightly, and then returns his attention to the keyboard.

"What's this you're working on?" Shultz asks.

"Oh," Stephen scratches his neck. "A friend of mine and I are planning on writing a book together. He'd sent me some of his writing, and I hadn't really given it the attention it deserves. I looked around for grammatical and spelling errors—you know, the usual stuff—but I hadn't really analyzed. I guess you could say I made a big mistake."

"What's that?" Shultz asks. He picks up the picture of Stephen and Phoebe. *When did they take a trip to the beach?*

"I didn't read it in context. I sort of looked at the words without really seeing the story," Stephen's comments line the margins of the word document.

"Well, that's good to hear. Which friend wrote this?"

"My friend Isaac."

"Right, I think you mentioned him before."

"I probably did. He's one of my best friends now," Stephen says.

"You haven't known him for that long."

"No, I really haven't. I got to know him over these past couple of months. He's one of the only people who ... who I feel I really *connect with*, you know what I mean?"

"No, I don't," Shultz shrugs.

"I have a lot of acquaintances. You're my best friend. We work together, we see each other pretty much every day. I still talk to people off and on who I knew in High School. But Isaac's different."

"How?"

"He just is. He's unafraid to let me into the worst parts of his life, and I guess I return the favor."

"That's commendable. That kind of transparency is extremely hard to find today," Shultz remarks.

"That's a true statement, Shultzy."

"I'm still mad at you."

"I'm sorry."

"Where's the alcohol?"

"Gone," Stephen feels his neck blotch. "It's gone. I stopped that."

"Thank the Lord. I was getting concerned."

"It wouldn't be us if we didn't concern each other once and a while."

"Oh, another thing, you know why I can't get mad at you too much?"

"Why's that?"

"Sales are increasing," Shultz says.

Stopping the scrolling of his mouse, Stephen asks, "Really?"

"Yeah. It was a blip. It was a small dip, but sales are back up now. We're not tanking after all. *Calls* is actually starting to pick up speed," Shultz claps Stephen on the shoulder, the same area where he'd been shot. "This might be massive after all, my man."

"Wow," Stephen says. "That's amazing."

"How are you doing, by the way?"

"I'm living," Stephen says. "That's all I can do."

"The fact you're back on track is extraordinary."

"You know me," Stephen lets the news of his book's recovery sink in. "I fall hard and bounce higher."

"You're an inspiration, my friend. I'm sorry I was so hard on you."

"You're my boss," Stephen snorts. "I was acting like a complete dickhead. You had every right to slap me down."

"Holy shit," Shultz says, leaping up from leaning on the desk.

"What?" Stephen jumps.

"Can I get that on a tape somewhere?"

"Ha-ha," Stephen sinks back into his chair. "I should've known you're being funny. You should sign up for some comedy shows. They'd be laughing at you, not with you."

"But I'd be making money," Shultz struts towards the door. "Nobody makes money in this publishing business."

"Yet somehow we're still here!" Stephen shouts after him. He returns his focus to the words on the page. The joy of being ahead of schedule gives him a warm glow.

I guess this is how to rebuild, Stephen thinks dimly. *Isaac's the one who I should be thanking, not who should be thanking me.*

The thoughts threaten to break through his demeanor, and Stephen shuts them off. He coughs, and lets his mind return to static as he closes the document with Isaac's words and continues on his Bessemer work. The static returns to his ears.

His focus is shattered by the fast return of Shultz, whose voice again brings him away from his work.

"Hey, Steve?"

Removing the earphones once again, Stephen responds, "Yes, boss?"

"I forgot to ask. Do you have any plans for dinner tonight?"

"Nope," Stephen sighs. He doesn't like going to restaurants alone.

"Good! You wouldn't mind coming to dinner with Jen and me, then?"

"Oh shit," Stephen says. "I get to actually interact with you in a place that isn't this office?"

"Very funny. Is that a yes?"

"Sure," Stephen stretches in his chair. "I need to get out a little bit."

"You're damn straight about that, mister."

"Where do you want to go?"

"How about the Hard Rock?" Shultz asks.

"You think we'll be able to get in there on a Wednesday night?"

"I don't see why not, as long as we leave early enough to avoid the traffic."

"That should be doable. It's on then."

"Is it a date?" Shultz chuckles.

"Sure, for you, it's a date."

"Perfect."

As Shultz strides happily out of the room, Stephen wonders exactly how long it's been since he went on a date with someone who cared.

[24]

There once was a young man who was betrothed by God to bring light to the blind. He was placed on the earth in the middle of a tumult of problems: violence, illness, poverty, classism, racism, xenophobia; all in the heartland, the epicenter, of one of the greatest nations in history. By rights, his story should be shouted from mountaintops, and proclaimed as an example of how those who fight for all they have, those who know the most darkness, are the ones who shine the brightest, laugh with the most meaning, turn conversations into opportunities to learn. Rising from the circumstances into which he was born, facing the lashes of those who claimed to love him, those in the society which was supposed to support him, he walked through the shadow of his own mind and he found a way to smile. The meaning was discovered in his creativity, in his desire to do good; he was going to be a nice person.

Lying on the bed in the hotel room, Isaac stares up at the ceiling. This place costs as much as half his rent for the month for a single night. Luckily, he'd planned ahead. He'd been fortunate enough to be blessed with the foresight to take his vacation in an organized fashion. The pleasant towels remain folded on the credenza, the flat-screen television dormant, the sheets on the bed undisturbed aside from the wrinkles which ripple out from his body. He's left his boots on. The only source of light in the room streams from the curtains leading to the small balcony; the night sky itself is beautiful, and Isaac wanted to see those stars. He'd always marveled at how the city below casts a glow from all the small bulbs, combining to break the absolution of the night. He'd been one of those tiny miracles once; humble, spiritual, someone who served. He'd given up his pulpit in the name of finding his own future. The rest of his walk has been all about forgiveness.

He's sinned.

The Devil, he knows, is a vicious and cunning serpent, who slithers through the rivers and channels to put his soul at risk, turning all he loves against him due to his reliance on the shrewd. The Devil had first appeared when he'd been 20, popping up in whispers which ruffled his skin in the dead of night with the warm breath of hell seeping from the floorboards. It'd told him to cast the child for whom he cared off of a bridge, to hang himself like an ornament from the ceiling, how the workers tying him up in the strait jacket in the mental hospital really were looking to set him alight. It'd told him to go home to God, that God is dead, God abandoned him in favor of a better alternative. Isaac closes his eyes. He knows the Devil surrounds him. It's not empirical; it's intrinsic. He'd been born with a mark, made to suffer, raised out of the womb of torment and despair against all the odds. The battles he's won, the times he's stood tall, come rushing to him. Those who he's lost and those who threw him away are now a chorus of voices, and they come not from the darkest pits, but from the open doors of the sky.

He's wanted to join them. He's wanted to tell God his gratefulness for his opportunity. He's tried to reach heaven before, but now is truly the time where his service concludes in humility, not humiliation.

Dully, Isaac turns to the nightstand. They've put out some quaint entertainment magazines, a remote control, and a couple of favors to make him feel at home.

He's not at home yet.

Reaching into his pocket, Isaac takes out his outdated, sleek black flip phone. A pang of regret reaches his ears, like an echoing piano in the fading notes of a song.

Turning on the screen, he opens his text messages. The screen freezes, because this thing is over seven years old. It loads, and Stephen's name pops up. Isaac checks the time—6:15. Steve's probably eating dinner. He's doing things Isaac should be doing. Lord knows he could be with Olivia right now, but he's not. He's the sin, he's the catalyst; he's the stain which God tried to wipe from the earth but could not cleanse.

She never asked for him. She never asked to be a witness to all four of the times he'd tried to quit. He's going to hurt a lot of people. That's how this is supposed to go, after all; the pain which bottles up, tears, rips, ravages and slices him shall be exploded and cast out into the world like a bomb. Eventually, in what's left behind, phoenixes will rise unburdened. Life, as they've all said, will go on. She'll find somebody who doesn't need medication, who can treat her how she deserves to be treated. His parents are already too blind, deaf, and ignorant to care; they know of the times he'd woken howling in the night, of the bills they've had to pay, how Satan truly works in the shadows. From the bottom of his aching bones, he's sorry.

Everybody reaches the end, don't they?

Selecting Stephen's name, Isaac writes the following words:

> *Hey, Steve. I need to talk to you when you have a minute*
> *my brother. Call me when you can.*

He's sorry he won't be able to see Stephen succeed. The man who saved his life is about to have his generosity returned unfulfilled, and that sucks. It sucks a lot. It sucks so much he almost regrets the fact the bottle of medication next to his bed is empty. If he were to have kept placing his doses in his mouth as needed to keep the voices out, he would've continued blocking God's voice. Instead, as he folds his hands over his chest and leans against the pillows, he knows that only He can truly judge what is best, and he hopes he's made Him proud, because, for all the love Isaac has known, he tried.

Jennifer Shultz probably should've become a model. For the life of him, Shultz can never believe how he got as lucky to have such a gorgeous brunette stoop so low as to marry a pompous ass with a little extra weight. Stephen knows that the story runs deeper, but for those seeing Shultz and Jen on one side of the table and Stephen sitting alone across from them, it sure seems as though the universe is askew.

"This is fitting," Shultz says. He's kept his gray blazer on from work, his chest hairs curling over his polo slightly.

"What?" Stephen asks, looking up from his menu. Various lyrics float to him from the ceiling, the annals of rock and roll preaching loudly in its sanctuary.

"A rock star sitting in a castle dedicated to rock stars," Shultz smirks. Jen slaps him quickly. She scoffs, and she addresses her husband's best man.

"Sorry, Steve. I truly apologize for his behavior," Jen says.

From behind the shield of his menu, Shultz laughs.

"Hey, I don't know, he's been quite feisty lately," Stephen flips the pages, the plastic bouncing.

"Oh, have I?" Shultz asks.

"Yes, you have. You almost fired me, after all."

"I think I probably should've, looking back at it."

"Yes, you should've. I also should've probably punched you in the face that time you brought that girl home drunk at three in the morning and proceeded to defile a perfectly clean set of white sheets with your filth," Stephen says.

Interrupted mid-drink, Shultz struggles not to spray the water across the table as he nearly chokes. Jen's face flushes as she places her head down, her expression contorted with mock shock.

"Oh *really* now?" She catches her breath. "You're saying Mr.

Patron Saint over here was a wild man in college?"

Shultz wipes his mouth with his napkin. "I can show you how much of a wild man I am now, give me some white sheets—I was the inspiration for *50 Shades*."

"Oh for the love of Christ," Stephen lowers his head behind his menu. "Maybe that's why Phoebe cheated on me, I didn't pay close enough attention to that book. She probably wanted to tie me up and flog me."

"Hey now, that requires communication!" Shultz says, winking.

"Right? I never did that. I never talked about anything," Stephen adjusts his silverware.

The three all look back to their choices, the words ringing in the air. Jen allows the silence to settle, and then her voice cuts the tension smoothly.

"Did you guys ever think of taking Bessemer global?" she asks.

"What, in this economy?" Shultz closes the menu with a puff of air.

"Yes, in this economy, darling."

"It'd be a thought. We now have the firepower to do it behind Mr. Christiansen over here," Shultz says, gesturing to Stephen.

"Please, Shultzy, don't screw with me." Stephen squints. *What in the hell is an Aerosmith Angus Burger?*

"Oh, I'm not screwing with you," Shultz lets the humor fade out of his voice. Jen and Shultz are both staring at Stephen. Stephen puts down the menu.

"Literally, if we keep selling like this, Stephen ... we're going to hit the Bestsellers list."

"Are you kidding me?" Stephen leans over the table. "Are you serious, Charlie?"

"Yup," Jen giggles. "He told me before we came here, so I knew you'd have that stupid look on your face."

"It's like after Phoebe originally agreed to go out with him back at UMBC. Congrats, kid, you made it," Shultz extends his hand, and

Stephen shakes it. In the middle of his rash of darkness, a small burst of fresh air has somehow survived.

He allows the news to embrace him, and he, like a family member reunited with a long lost relative, can only smile in shock.

"That's complete insanity. When did you hear the news?"

"Yesterday," Shultz knocks the chunks of ice in his glass around with his straw. "Now, I'd ask for liquor, but knowing you you'd probably knock it all over the office again. I'm toasting to you tonight. You did this. You built this. This is your victory."

"No, Charlie, it's ours," Stephen feels as if the air around him is laced with the scent of joy. *The New York Times' Bestsellers?*

"And no," Jen says. "We didn't buy the copies."

A buzz breaks the mood. Stephen removes his phone and looks down.

"I'll be back in a second, I need to take this," Stephen tells them.

"Who is it?" Shultz asks. "Someone telepathically hear the news already?"

"Nah, its Isaac. He needs me to call him."

"Ah, alright," Even as Shultz says it, Stephen is already walking towards the door.

"Wait, Steve, what should we order you?" Shultz calls after him.

Past the radius of the words, Stephen doesn't turn.

Shultz and Jen share a glance. They don't know.

[25]

Baltimore opens up before him, with sirens, voices, and different lives all triggering his senses. There are no more hidden truths of the world; there is nothing more to be found.

"Hey, Isaac?"

"Hello, Stephen," The call quality is impeccable.

"What's going on?"

"Not much. I'm planning on going to sleep."

Stephen looks down at his watch. A happy family of four passes him, walking in front of the bench on which he sits. They're bubbly kids, and their laughter echoes.

"It's only 6:17, my man, why so early tonight?" Stephen asks.

"I'm tired."

"Was it a long day at work?"

"Yup."

"They finally let you move away from all the people so the voices wouldn't be as severe, right?"

"Yeah. They let me do a lot of the manual labor in the back, let me stack some boxes. It drains you real quick, though."

"I can imagine," Stephen sits back on the wood, staring at the remnants of the sun still lingering in the brilliant twilight sky. "I couldn't spend my days carrying all that stuff."

"That's not what I mean," Isaac chuckles.

"Hm?"

"It drains you, like you said. It drains you when you're the only one, when you're constantly fighting yourself, when the very things you grow up being taught to avoid constitute who you are."

All of the people around him disappear, along with the chill of the wind. A frozen sweat spreads across the back of his neck.

"Isaac ... are you alright?"

"Yes, I'm fine. Don't worry about me."

"Where's Olivia?"

"She's at home."

"And where are you?"

"In bed."

"In bed where?"

Straining to listen, Stephen attempts to coax an answer.

"Isaac, where are you?"

"Stephen, I need you to calm down. I'm fine. I'm perfectly fine."

"Have you been taking your medication?"

"Yes."

"Are you lying to me?"

"Not at all, my friend. You are the one person who I will not lie to."

"What does that mean?"

"Stephen," Isaac's voice is calm, but heightened in urgency. "Where are *you* right now?"

"I'm outside the Hard Rock Cafe."

"Then please don't be making a scene over me, of all people."

The concrete below him is pallid as the phone shakes in his hand.

"Now, I want to tell you something." Isaac continues.

"Alright," Stephen sits back. "But you need to promise me you're ok. Does Olivia know where you are?"

The line is silent.

"Isaac? Does Olivia know where you are?"

"It's odd, man."

"Answer me," Stephen presses.

"It's really, really odd."

"God *dammit* Isaac, does Olivia know where you are?" Stephen stands, glancing fervently around him. A man walking by jumps, his white beard tingling, his surprise turning to condemnation as he continues on his way.

"Olivia is fine. She's always been fine. It's me who's been the broken one."

Slumping back down to the bench, Stephen can't reply.

"And that's what I wanted to ask you, my friend," Isaac says the words almost lazily.

"Isaac ... don't do this."

"Do what? Like I said, I'm going to sleep."

"Ok, so you're going to sleep, and your fiancée has no idea where you are, you won't tell me where you are, and you're speaking with really weighted words."

"Like I said, my friend, I'm fine. I'm tired. Don't go worrying yourself about me, ok? And that's what I really want to know, what would truly help me sleep better tonight, and why I called you—why do you care about me?"

"What?" Stephen's tone is incredulous. "What do you mean?"

"When we met, you were an idol of mine. You were, and still are, somebody who I wish to emulate in every facet of my craft. You had everything. You're in a position in society where somebody like me is less than nothing, where I don't matter, where you can turn away and ignore me like I've been ignored all my life. I've been trampled on, punched, kicked, spit on, pissed on, rejected, and degraded by all of those who had the chance to inflict the blows—why didn't you?"

"Why are you asking me this?"

"I need to know."

If he's in a hotel, it has to be nearby. It has to be downtown, right? The inner harbor? Could he have gone to Towson?

"Take your time," Isaac smirks.

"I—I don't know. I saw somebody who needed my help."

"But why? You could've kept walking."

"I could've."

"But you didn't."

"But I didn't."

"Because?"

"Because I care," Stephen feels tears sneaking out, and he blinks rapidly, his face crumbling. He sits down on the bench, his breath coming in bursts, and it takes a few seconds for him to regain his composure.

"Mr. Christiansen," Isaac laughs lowly. "You are one of God's angels."

"No, I'm not, Isaac. I'm somebody who tries to do the right thing. This world is fucked up. This world is completely fucked up."

"Oh, I'm aware," Isaac says. "It's the kind of place where we don't say something until it's too late, where we are always looking for answers, for easy opportunities, for fast decisions which will solve problems quickly. We divide people into spectrums of race, color, creed, and religion, and we compartmentalize compassion to an action to be put on a resume. We see people only for their homelessness, we categorize people into social classes which aren't supposed to touch for fear of consequences we invent. We decry mental illness because we don't understand it, we perpetuate inequality because we're scared of it, we go through our lives running from everything we don't want to acknowledge so we can escape the burden of caring."

Isaac takes a deep breath, and then he continues.

"There were, statistically, over a dozen people within earshot of that confrontation that day, Mr. Christiansen. And you stepped in and got called crazy. You stepped over the limitations of your own personal safety in the name of helping another, to challenge the quotas of who should be cared about and who should be seen as a number. You transcended the ideas which divide our humanity, and somehow, by a miracle, an affluent author was able to somehow befriend the wreck who now calls you a hero." Isaac's voice falters, and Stephen hears what sound like little puffs of wind—sobs.

"Isaac, no. I honestly did what I would've wanted someone to do for me, and I never thought I'd be lucky enough to meet someone as brave as you."

Cars whisk down the city streets. Baltimore's always been known as a place with charm.

"I'm not brave," Isaac mutters.

"Yes you are. You're the bravest man I've ever known."

"You should probably meet more people."

"Listen, I want you to call Olivia. Tell her where you are."

"She doesn't need to worry anymore, my friend. Neither do you. Nobody needs to worry, I know I'm certainly not going to."

"What does that mean?"

"You are going to wake up tomorrow, and you're going to keep moving on. I'm going to go to sleep soon, and I'm going to rest."

"What the hell does that mean, Isaac?"

"What? It means I'm going to bed. I've had such a long day of working," His voice wavers over the line in small crescendos.

"Ok," Stephen says. "Ok, but you need to promise me one thing, alright?"

"Anything for you, my friend."

"When you wake up in the morning, you're going to give me a call?"

"But that's what I called to tell you."

"What?"

"I'm ok. I'm fine. You don't need to worry anymore. I've beaten the demons."

"I don't want to lose you, Isaac. I can't lose you."

"You'll never lose me, unless you forget me."

Planting his head in his hands, Stephen's fingers clutch his cropped hair.

A few seconds pass in silence.

"I'm going to let you go now, Steve." Isaac's voice is layered, saturated with fatigue.

"Alright. You call me."

"I want to tell you one more thing."

"Sure," Stephen looks at the people laughing in the shops across the street, the vehicles gleefully running down the avenue.

"I used to be part of a congregation."

"Right, you've told me."

"I used to live in a home which held me, and my family. Also, in a home with Olivia."

"Yes."

"I work in a factory which houses almost 500 employees."

A fresh tear crescents its way out of Stephen's eye, a raindrop on a windshield.

"I live in a city which holds over six-hundred-thousand people. We live in a country with over three-hundred and sixty-five million souls. We live in a world with seven billion stories, all drifting forward into the ethers of the future restlessly."

Collapsing on himself, Stephen hunches over. People stop to peer at him peculiarly, some potentially recognizing his face from his books.

"You know what I've learned, Mr. Christiansen?"

With his voice lost in the turning of the world, Stephen listens.

"It takes a crowd of people to know you're truly alone."

Faintly, the call disconnects. Stephen dully recognizes his phone dropping to the pavement, its transparent screen protector shattering. The doors to the Hard Rock swing open as Shultz rushes out, and he will remember looking up at his friend and being unable to utter a word. Shultz puts his arm around him, distantly asking *what's wrong*, and Stephen, for all the books written, letters sent, entries penned, manuscripts reviewed, and words used, cannot find a single syllable.

[26]

They found him sleeping.

In the early morning hours they'd entered his room, the discarded bottle of medication ready for a refill. The bullet which had struck Stephen in the shoulder finally found its mark in the smiling face now free of pain. All of the scars which cover his body, and the ones under his skin, are gone. They're saying the cause of death is the very medication which was supposed to save him. They're saying the reason he's no longer alive is due to the very heart which was supposed to sustain him finally resting. They found his emergency contact information easily after they identified him, and the cell phone he'd used hours earlier would be utilized for the psychological autopsy. Nobody had to be responsible for him now. None need carry the guilt associated with his passing, as if he'd stepped in front of a train or car. There's no more reason for him to have to be an infinite expense in a world where monetary value is an easy answer to a person's worth.

He's passing with no hatred, with all the forgiveness possible.

He only sees light now.

The weight has been lifted.

[27]

November 21st, 2014

No results.

Adding the word *obituary* to the query, Stephen hits enter again; the same screen pops up.

When are obituaries usually published? I know Phoebe's came out three days later.

He scrolls down the page, finding only links he's clicked before and the public parts of Isaac's life. It's all old news, and he can't satiate the gnawing feeling in his stomach.

Insanely, he attempts the same search.

Isaac Sellers.

YouTube, Sound Cloud, Google Plus, WordPress.

Isaac Sellers Baltimore Obituary.

Only the aforementioned pages sneak out of the web's bulwark.

Isaac Sellers suicide.

Tauntingly, the results returned on the earlier searches again are at the forefront of any and all answers, which only cause the rift to deepen.

Deleting all the terms in the search bar leaves a screen of icy white. Sitting on the cushions, recently placed back in the nooks of the couch, he leans back with his hands covering his mouth. They taste of guilt for the second time in as many months, for he knows what's occurred. He prays his fear is a misconception. The blood of Phoebe is not yet dry; Isaac is the next to be lost due to Stephen's inability to make a decision to change the future. Full bottles of liquor lined the trash bags this morning; tea bottles sit in the cabinets of the kitchen. No sound comes from the television, and the pictures flash in a gray sequence; slideshows of tragedy, puppies, and feel-good stories at noon on a Friday.

His phone's off. That's why it's going right to voicemail.

Shultz understands why he's off today. Stephen doesn't. After dinner last night, Shultz had suggested he take a moment to quell his paranoia. Now he sits surrounded by the creeping thoughts, their spectral and aching bodies filling his lungs with imaginary smoke and his willpower shackled to a miracle.

A knock comes from the front door.

Startled, Stephen whips around to the foyer, and for only a split second, he knows who's going to be standing behind that patch of wood. He'll greet him with a hug and a huge smile. Stephen rises from the couch. With the steps across the floor, he's tracing the same path he'd expected to walk when Phoebe said she'd been leaving, that perhaps all of the negativity and destruction in the world are simply nightmares escaped from their cages. His hand rests upon the cool doorknob, and without thinking to look through the peephole, he turns and pulls the door open.

Outside, the world's glare hits him, and for a millisecond, he doesn't see who's waiting on the porch.

Believe.

She's shorter than he imagined, with the same dark skin as Isaac and the lies of hope's marks still on her face. Her black hair runs down to the small of her back, a white coat shielding her from the waning autumn wind. The expression on her face is a hodgepodge of doom and appreciation.

"Hello," She says timidly, her shin-high boots scraping the welcome mat on the floor.

"Good morning," Stephen's words are as automatic as a dispenser.

"You're Stephen," she says. "Stephen Christiansen." Her voice is both a statement and a question.

"Yes, I am."

"I'm sorry to intrude on you like this."

"Please."

They stare at each other. A singsong cry of a siren peels down the street.

"Do you know who I am?" she asks.

Stephen nods.

"Do you know why I'm here?"

The truth is made flesh, and Stephen nods again.

She smiles, and a tear creases her cheek.

Wordlessly, they embrace, with the facade of total strangers falling.

"I'm sorry this place is so wrecked. I had a bit of an accident," Stephen hands her a glass, one of the few which hadn't been broken in the aftermath of Phoebe's death. Graciously, blending into the couch, Olivia Sellers takes the cold water and sips it gently. After a couple of seconds, she places it down on the coffee table.

Even though he's not thirsty, Stephen drains the entire glass. She sits like Isaac does—or, as he *did*—with her hands folded in her lap and her posture respectful, cautious.

"I'm so terribly sorry."

"Thank you," Olivia whispers. "It hasn't hit me yet."

"It doesn't." Stephen says.

"I'm sorry for you as well. I know it's hardly even been a month since you lost Phoebe."

"Thanks," Stephen pushes down the implosion, triggered only by sentiments of others. *Not now.* "I only knew Isaac for a couple of months, but he was one of the best friends I've ever had. He inspired me every day."

"You inspired him, honestly," Olivia shifts on the couch. "He talked about your writing, he said he was going to be sitting with me one day and we'd see you on the Oprah show and laugh."

Despite everything, the words elicit a small grin from the author.

"I told him to stop saying that. My ego really doesn't need any more inflation."

"You don't have an ego," Olivia says, shaking her head.

"Oh yes, I do."

"Really? I never heard about it."

"Isaac was special. He saw through it. It's odd to say how some random guy who I prevented from being robbed became a brother, but I am so unbelievably thankful."

"So am I. If you hadn't stepped in, we wouldn't have been able to afford any more medication for him, at least until the next month."

"I think he told me that."

A respectful lull clears the air prior to Stephen's next question.

"What happened to him?"

Taking another sip, Olivia sighs.

"They found him yesterday morning. He'd rented a hotel for the night, told me that he'd had to work overtime and was going to be late, said they'd booked him for a double shift. He's always enjoyed taking the overtime due to the extra money. He told me not to worry, but of course I worried. After he still wasn't home by two in the morning—I'd stayed up waiting—I called in and asked one of his friends who he worked with where he'd gotten to, and he told me that he hadn't even come into work that day. At that point, I knew something was terribly wrong, and I called the police. They tracked him down and ... well, he was sleeping. They said it looked like he'd been in the bed for at least six, maybe seven hours. They found the empty bottle of his medication next to the bed, along with a note for me."

An army of ice engulfs Stephen, and he shudders as if he's been cast into the middle of winter without a home.

"He'd called three people prior to going to sleep that night. A friend he met online, his sister, and you."

"Was I the last person to talk to him?"

"No," Olivia says. "The last one he called was his sister. You were first. He didn't call me because he knew I'd stop him. I'd been the one to find him the other four times he'd tried, and I guess he knew this time that he couldn't do that again. In his mind ... he was always so hurt ... he didn't want to burden me with being the one to actually find him. The police were the ones who broke into the room in order to put the pieces together."

"So I was one of the last people he talked to," Stephen allows the words to hang, not directed at anyone in particular.

"Yes. That's one of the reasons I'm here. I didn't talk to him at all that day, besides when he said goodbye in the morning. If you don't mind, I'd like to ask exactly what he said."

The response is quickly recalled, data newly collected and highly important.

"He said he was tired."

"He said that a lot."

"He said he had a hard day at work, and he was looking to sleep, and he told me not to worry. I saw it as cryptic, but he'd told me stuff like this a lot when we'd talk. He helped me navigate my own maze, as usual, with my grief and my work and my problems. He was so burdened, yet he always looked to focus on other people's issues instead of his own."

"That's Isaac," Olivia laughs, her humor vacant.

"I got extremely concerned afterwards, but I didn't have your number. I knew he was in a hotel in Baltimore, but there was nothing I could do."

"You weren't supposed to do anything."

"But I could've."

"No."

The issue is settled for a moment in Stephen's silence.

"You did so much for him, Stephen."

The empty television taunts him. *The Oprah Show! I'll say I knew that guy!*

"He left something for you, as well."

"He did?"

"Yes." Olivia reaches into her coat and pulls out a slip of paper, folded.

"I found this with your name on it. He made a batch of them, apparently, and left them on his desk. I didn't think to touch them until after ... until after. I didn't open it. The words are for you."

The paper is coarse under Stephen's fingers, and he places it on the coffee table gingerly, as if it's apt to crumble and fall apart at the slightest burst of wind.

"Thank you, Olivia."

Olivia says, "Thank you for being his friend."

The paper is folded, sealed with a small, golden sticker of a tree.

She leaves ten minutes later, giving him her number so they can stay in touch. She's on to spread the news to those who need to know, collecting the pieces of a tragedy; only after the months pass and the shock fades will the pain be allowed to run its course.

Sitting in his place on the couch, Stephen's hands tremor.

Hey Stephen. You'll be disappointed in me, but I just couldn't handle the stress, anxiety or pain in my life. I had to do it, and I hope you know that you were a great inspiration and friend that I very so needed. Thanks for the time you've spent in my life, you are one of a kind.

Blinking, Stephen's laptop screensaver is a picture of the Baltimore harbor.

[28]

December 21st, 2006

The field is a sea of reflections, popping into the winter air with the drifting Christmas music's bells. Couples of all kinds walk the paths between trees entwined with strands of beaming red and cheerful green. Laughter breaks the suffocation of the chill, with the snow of January still to come. Houses, cut and pasted out of show-tunes and Rudolph the Red Nosed Reindeer, shadow the figures strolling together, the coldness an excuse for a hug. A scent of happiness drifts from the evergreen trees, their needles holding the strands of decorations basking and glinting in the austere of the friendly moon. Each breath from the couples contributes to such a vocation, one of secluded, simple joy.

He's never been a strapping young man, and she's never cared about that. They'd known each other first as peers, then classmates, then friends, then lovers; that evolution completes as he looks down into her eyes. He'd first noticed them when they'd sat across the room from each other in the Introductory Writing class last year, and he'd mustered up the courage to allow all the theories in his head to be tested by reality. He'd decided to take a chance on tangibility despite the fact he's been scorned and burnt by life. He knows his challenge is to overcome the hurt, surpass the hatred for the person he's been, and now not to be jaded towards the young woman who snuggles against the arm of his jacket. His responsibility is one of individuality, one which is lonely being the only kid who hasn't drank or done drugs in his group of friends. Lord knows Charlie's been out the entire night. This woman doesn't care. She's still by his side, and she almost presses against the small box which hides inside his coat, waiting for the perfect moment.

"Look at that, Steve!" Phoebe points as a small child, dressed as a reindeer in a green sweater with soft antlers, dashes by them.

"I wasn't expecting to see a reindeer," Stephen replies. "I thought they only existed in cartoons and in Canada."

"He's so cute," she muses. As they walk, he feels her hand squarely in his, the warmth overpowering the nip of the wind. "I remember being that age," Phoebe says. Stephen's sweater is doing a good job of masking the slight perspiration of his skin. "I probably ran the same path he's running now." Phoebe looks at the trees around her. All different specimens of foliage and agriculture inhabit Peddler's Village, Pennsylvania, with some dominating the onlooker in sheer beauty as their smaller cousins capture holiday wishes and expel Christmas cheer as oxygen.

"Were you as much of a hellion at his age?" Stephen grins.

"I'm still a hellion now," Phoebe pinches his hand, and he pulls away in mock pain.

"Ow! Jesus, you don't have to remind me."

Soon they're joined again, and the clutter of the village opens into an expanse of a small field, where couples may gaze up at the unfolding universe.

"Do you want to go into the field and look at all the pretty stars?" Stephen turns in the direction of the grass, his face accenting his exaggerated excitement.

"How'd you know?" Phoebe's sarcasm playfully nudges him.

In the center, floating above the ground, the lights from the bulbs on the trees and the stars' longevity meet to connect the earth and sky. All of the luminosity from below pales in comparison to the gorgeousness of a world not dominated by pollution, simply open and awaiting the curious. Other stargazers sit on blankets. To dissect the wonders of the night is a simple concept, yet so elusive. Phoebe and Stephen always enjoy the atypical, knowing in their oddity they're allowed to be genuine. While the evening is a gnawing cold, they huddle close together on the dry ground. The grass of the knolls in the field slopes downwards, forming perfect theatre seats to the eternally shifting stage above them. As they sit, nestled underneath a solitary tree at the top of the hill, Phoebe presses herself gently into Stephen's chest, their backs supported by the incline of the soft grass.

"What do you think is out there?" Phoebe asks, blinking slowly, a stupid smile on her face. Death would be acceptable with the quality of this moment.

Space stretches out before Stephen welcomingly as he stares into the rotating arcs of the earth.

"I don't know."

"Aliens?" Phoebe shifts closer to him. "God?"

"Maybe. Could be both, you never know."

In the distance, a carol begins, singing about the luckiness of life.

"How are you tonight, Ms. Walker?" Stephen peers at her. She's focused on the celestial, a blissful gleam to her expression.

"I'm perfect," She turns to him.

"Perfect?"

"Perfect," she repeats.

"I don't know how you could be more perfect."

"I can't. This is it, right here," She assures him.

"You sure you don't want anything else that's out there? There's a lot more. People with bigger houses, bigger lives, bigger dreams."

"I don't need them."

"I'm pretty shaky. I don't really have a plan. I've got big goals and a small wallet," Stephen feels his pulse quicken as the questions meant to dissuade her fall to the correct answers.

"I love you," She shrugs. "That's all that really matters."

"I love you too. But I'm saying; I'm not very popular. I'm not very good looking."

"Stop it," Phoebe says, elbowing him in the ribs. Her jab catches the box hiding inside the fabric of his coat.

"I'm serious. I'm weird. I'm not looking to go out and party with Charlie, or maybe become a businessman, and I'm not too conservative. I'm either going to chase this whole writing dream or die trying."

"And I'm going to be with you," Phoebe adjusts herself, and her lovely hair touches his cheek. The nervousness falls away like a descending stream of water into a pond. Peace washes over his muscles, and he feels the small box suddenly asking to move.

"Charlie wants to be a publisher, you know," Stephen reaches into his pocket, and he removes the box carefully. Phoebe doesn't stir; she laughs a laugh which fills the air, prettier to him than any song.

"He's got crazier dreams than you do. There's no money in book publishing, as far as I've heard."

"Well, that's the thing," his voice is low. "We're all works in progress. Life is a road, and those who we love are happy accidents."

"Poetic," Phoebe chuckles. Stephen shifts, and then he stands. Phoebe sits up, looking at him.

"Follow me," He stretches out a hand, the other held behind his back.

"What? I was getting comfortable!"

"Come on, it'll only take a minute. I want to check out this tree up here."

Rolling her eyes, Phoebe stands, and then stumbles a tad. Stephen catches her, preventing her from tumbling down the hill. In seconds, the two are holding each other softly in the comedy of the moment.

"Don't be so clumsy," Stephen chides. He's standing close enough to see her cheeks attempting to imitate the color of her hair.

"I'm such a mess," Phoebe looks around. None of the other couples noticed. The top of the hill underneath the branches is devoid of tourists. The closest pedestrians are sprawled on a blanket at least thirty feet downrange.

"You're my mess," Stephen practically drags her up the hill, playfully acting as if he's waiting for her to fall again. "But that means I don't want to clean you up if you trip and bust your head."

"Asshole," Phoebe mutters.

Stephen reaches the base of the tree, its confident trunk vibrant with age. The branches overhead bear a welcoming aura.

Phoebe, using her arms as balance, walks to stand beside him as he gazes up at the limbs.

"Why did we walk up here, again? Do you suddenly want to become a botanist? Are you inspecting for blight?"

He turns to her, and the look on his face takes her breath.

"Phoebe Michelle Walker," he says. Carefully, she falls silent. He steps close to her.

"When I first met you," he clears his throat, and the words are no longer a whisper. "I was broken. My mom's been gone for six years; I hadn't been able to fully recover from all that went wrong. My dad never put me in therapy. I didn't have friends in high school to listen. I came to you, and I remember the first day I saw you, you were the most beautiful girl I'd ever imagined. But that isn't why I started dating you, why I collapsed into you with the vulnerability I thought would be a weakness to show. I love you not because you're absolutely drop dead stunning, but because you take the doubt and the weakness of my soul and turn it into confidence, because you complete something which I lost that I didn't even know was missing, and because I want to see your dreams become realities, see your hopes be fulfilled, see you be everything you ever could be because you are who you are," The nervousness recedes, and the soft exterior of the box in his hand caresses the flatness of his palm. "I want to build a life with you, far past school, beyond dates, a transcendence of this world where finding love is a miracle. Above every single goal I've ever had, I want to see you smile like we've smiled tonight, and I want to use the opportunities for which I've fought so hard to make our time on this earth mean something."

He drops down to one knee in the grass, and her hand moves to her mouth, her eyes opening wide, the realization hitting them like a falling star crashing into the earth in a brilliant blaze. After days of hibernation, the compact, velvet box opens to reveal a stunning diamond ring, selected with the assistance of Phoebe's sister Grace a month ago, all of Stephen's savings expressed in a single band of radiant silver. The diamond set in the center glints in the duality of the lights from the ground and the distance above.

"Phoebe," Stephen asks. "Will you marry me?"

For a second, the question shoots up into the stratosphere, the compounded doubts of Stephen's entire mortality rushing out in a charged exhale.

"Yes," She says softly.

"You will?" Stephen removes the ring from the box and takes her outstretched hand.

"Yes," She says, louder now, beaming in elated stupidity. "Yes!"

Carefully, he places the ring on her finger, and as it slides into place, what he'd known to be life up and through that moment disappears; and all he needs exists in the hysterically happy woman who now jumps onto him. They fall backwards under the shade of the tree, and she's kissing him like she's never kissed him before, the grass underneath them breaking the fall with magic all around them. Two lives became one.

In a far off apartment in Baltimore, somewhere beyond their point of reference, perhaps a man and a woman with a completely different story are scraping together the ability to eat on that night, similarly recently engaged.

Maybe the demons of the world they're facing are expelled not by fields of lights, but by the simplicity of being together against all the odds, past the shackles of mental illness and a lack of self-esteem—because we treasure those we love.

[29]

February 20th, 2015

Three raps sound from the closed door; Shultz looks up from his computer tacitly. He'd been daydreaming watching the stock markets. Prince Harry is dating Emma Watson, according to Facebook. It's hilarious how the cosmos turns impossibilities into common sense.

"Come in," Shultz calls, clicking away from Facebook and back to a document tracking the company's sales. *If these keep increasing on this incline, then we'll turn the largest quarter margin in our history.*

The door opens. Stephen rounds the corner swiftly, looking up from the ground as he crosses the threshold. His suit is tightly pressed, a gray jacket adorning a white collared shirt. His face is shaven, his skin reservedly pale, brimming like a rebuilt suit of armor. He strolls across the carpet and takes a seat in one of the two posh chairs in front of Shultz's desk. Shultz nods as he enters, pushing back from his desk to place his dress shoes on top of the mahogany.

"So, I see you own the place now, huh?" Shultz chews on the capped end of his pen.

"Sometimes, I think I do," Stephen says.

Tossing the pen onto his desk, Shultz says, "With the upgrades we've had recently thanks to your book sales, I guess I do owe you something."

Taking a look at the calendar which adorns Shultz's desk, Stephen nods.

"What?" Shultz asks.

Falling to darkness like a field under a twilit sky, Stephen's face doesn't crack.

"It's been four months today," he states.

"Wow," Shultz remarks. "It has?"

"Yup. Four months since Phoebe," Stephen rips his train of thought from the tunnel before the memories can overtake him. He's becoming adept at managing the swirling absence.

"I still can't believe it," Shultz takes his feet off the desk. He closes the lid of his laptop, wheeling in to see his friend clearly. "I also can't believe how well you're handling it."

"Thanks," Stephen says quickly.

"Is there anything I can help with?" Shultz asks.

"No thanks, Charlie. That's not why I'm here."

"Oh?" Shultz leans in quizzically.

"It's also been three months," Stephen brushes the front of his dress pants.

"Three months?"

"Since Isaac."

Cold, gripping realization snares Shultz.

"Oh my god. Was it really exactly a month apart?"

"Yup," Stephen's either going to smile at that or cry. He elects to smile.

"I don't know what to say," Shultz's voice is distant.

"That's a first," Stephen quips.

"I'm sorry, Stephen."

"So am I," Stephen coughs. "But that's also not why I'm here. Well, it kind of is."

"Alright," Shultz sits up straighter.

"I know I haven't told you about this," Stephen begins. "But I had to keep it a secret."

"Okay," Shultz raises an eyebrow.

"I've been working on something."

"You have?"

"Yes."

"Since?"

"December. It took me a couple tries to start but I have it now."

"What? Are you talking about a novel?"

Collecting his thoughts by staring at the ceiling, Stephen turns his gaze back down to Charlie after a few seconds.

"Before he passed, Isaac sent me a manuscript."

"I recall you mentioning he'd written."

"Yes. He knew who I was before we met. He knew my writing. He saw me as an idol, and then we bonded through mutual love of our craft. He showed me a universe I'd never known before. In the middle of my own reeling pain, I was able to finally put myself in somebody else's shoes. I'd never been able to do that before."

"What do you mean?" Shultz asks, squinting like he's staring at the sun.

"Shultzy, we were affluent white pricks who went to college. Some people never get that opportunity."

"I never thought of you that way," Shultz says.

"I know you didn't, but that isn't the point. The point is I saw a window into the world I could've never hoped to experience anywhere else, and it ... it changed me. It changed me a whole lot, and it's been a reference point which has kept me from going under after losing Phoebe, and also losing him so soon after. There have been nights where I've been drowning in my own questions, and it's the memory of this man which inspires me to push on."

A man shouts from the street outside, something about discounted prices on lunch at the sub shop across the street.

"I'm sorry to hear you were in such an awful place, Steve, but it's ... expected after the weight which has been dropped on you recently," Shultz says.

The only acknowledgement from Stephen is the look in his eyes.

"Before he died," Stephen says. "We talked about writing a book based on his life. To tell his story, to use the events which shaped him as a symbol for good in a world run by ignorance."

"That's amazing," Shultz says.

"It would've been. Unfortunately, he died before we could start working on it."

"What a shame," Shultz shakes his head.

"But ..." Stephen says.

"But what?" Shultz leans over his desk.

"But I still had the work he sent me."

"Ah," Shultz's face blanks. "What was it?"

"A collection of writing. It wasn't very long, only around 20,000 words detailing everything from his musings on life and his trials with schizophrenia to how his fiancée, Olivia, acted as a guiding force."

Clearing his throat, Stephen speaks words of unfiltered truth.

"Isaac was the most courageous man I've ever known."

Shultz waits.

"He sounds like he was a truly benevolent soul," Shultz says.

"He is."

It's coming; Stephen's been building to something, the dramatist still intact.

"I went back and looked over his work. I talked to Olivia. I reflected on the kind of person I knew him to be, and I realized this: I am not the one to tell his story," Stephen crosses his arms. "I can't tell his story. I don't know the details. It's not my place to air the truth of the hardships only partially told, and it's not my place to take their entire family history and reveal it to the world."

"Completely understandable," Shultz prepares himself.

"But I could tell how he impacted my story," Stephen gives a miniscule smile. "I could talk about how this man who I met guided me through uncertain waters from his experience, how in the midst of his own tragedies and awful days he brought me a bright spot when I needed it most, and how he was, unquestionably, the bravest man I ever knew. I could make a gift for somebody who deserves to be remembered, because he was different, Charlie."

A sudden and immense sense of pride triggers a smile from the director.

"So, what are you saying, Mr. Christiansen?"

Stephen reaches into his pocket and removes a flash drive.

"I have a manuscript I'd like to submit."

[30]
The Theory of Talking to Trees

An excerpt from the upcoming novel by
Baltimore's own Stephen Christiansen

I'll revisit that spot in front of the harbor sometimes.

*I'll pretend he's going to walk down the opposite path to meet me. It'll
be a cold day, perhaps with the echoes of the splashing water around us,
with the kids paddling in their boats, playing war across the waves. He'll
walk up to me and give me a firm handshake and a hug, smiling broader
than the Chesapeake Bay Bridge.*

*We'll stand there and say how fortunate we are to be together again. It
seemed as if the last time we talked was eons ago, in a different galaxy, in
a universe where things made sense and we could solve all the problems of
the world through a simple conversation on a Friday, Saturday, Sunday,
or even a Monday. After he'd pulled through his shifts at the factory where
he lived and died for his money, he'd always have time to hear about how I
was tired. After he'd told me about the ways in which he'd walked through*

the snow in his flip flops, and how he'd felt the sting of defeat his entire life, he'd hear about my victories without jealousy. He'd always find a way to show empathy, to give when so much had been taken from him, and not to hold a grudge. No matter how much was thrown at him, he always fought through it and found a way to make my days better. The last time we met on the harbor's edge, it'd been after my fiancée died, and I was on the brink of following her. Then a man with four suicide attempts to his name taught me the importance of life.

We'll stand there and we'll find answers to questions which we were scared to ask. We'd talk about the point of hoping anymore when everything that'd been promised to us never arrived, and how we never caught the things we chased after. We'd talk about how beautiful the good looks in a world which wants to destroy us, and we'd speak feverishly about how, together, we navigated the rough acts of the currents like we were skilled sailors. The kind of spirit the man carried with him is beyond all comprehension, but to give you an idea, he still found a way to cheer me up after the medication he took to stop the voices from his schizophrenia made him suicidal. To call him a magician implies he used tricks. To call him courageous insults his spirit by trying to capture it in one word.

I could've reached out to him, not been so consumed by my own pain to forget how much he'd been hurting, and I imagine often if things would be different if I could've done something.

I know I'll meet him again.

We'll talk like we used to. I'll tell him how valuable the knowledge he gave me has been over the years since we saw each other last, and he'll say he's been honored to have been lucky enough to help me.

We'll stand around for a while. We'll go back to our own lives. We'll be old friends, and he'll talk about how after all he's seen, he's not downtrodden, defeated, or broken—he's lucky to have his wife and to have woken up on another morning.

I'll meet him someday. I don't know when it'll be, but after all he's done for me, the ways he's broadened my horizons, the way he's cared for me using the quality of our time over the quantity, he'll turn to me and say,

"Thank you."

And with that, he'll walk down the street under the incandescent lights, slowly moving from the world we shared, with all the burdens we shouldered and hopes we tended, the failures surpassed and victories earned, until he becomes a shining spot amongst the blackness, heading towards the future, carried off by the wind of a chilly November evening.

I don't know when I'll see him again, but I'll walk down to that spot by the harbor sometimes, think of him, and smile.

I'll be waiting.

Acknowledgments

Thank you to Nate for your courage, your friendship, and for the way you lived, which shattered my affluence and inspires me constantly. Thank you to Chantel, and Judith, for your correspondence regarding this project.

Thank you to my friends and family who supported me as I wrote this story, and whose compassion and grace are the wealth of my life: my father, my Aunts and Uncles, my cousins, my grandmother, my Opa, and my good friends Gary, Keith, Justin, Luke, Shelby, Emily, Jill, and Joey. I owe a huge debt to my friend Blake for critiquing the manuscript. Last, but absolutely never least, thank you to my mother for teaching me to be unafraid to care about other people.

A huge thank you to Dr. Matt Hobson of Loyola University Maryland for his creatively constructive criticism; my gratitude to you for your honesty and developmental expertise! Thank you to Professor Nina Guise-Gerrity for your interest in my work and for supporting all of my creative endeavors.

I would also like to thank the Writing Center Practice and Theory class of Loyola University Maryland: Dr. Lisa Zimmerelli, Amy, Brian, JoJo, Chris, Madison, Jamie, Emily, Ellen, Janae, and Tanique (in order of where we sat in class!). In our class's discussion regarding issues of the world, we came together as 11 students in a gorgeously poignant way. You all hold the wealth of the future in your hands, and

I know you'll do the most you can with what has been given to you.

My deepest gratitude to Dr. Kevin Atticks of Apprentice House Press, as well as the students in the Manuscript Evaluation course, for accepting this novel for publication. Thank you for believing.

To anyone who reads this novel, thank you.

About the Author

Karl Dehmelt is currently enrolled at Loyola University Maryland in Baltimore, Maryland. He is the author of *The Hard Way Back to Heaven* (Apprentice House, 2015). A lifelong writer, he strives to honor his family, friends, and those he cares about in everything he does.

Apprentice House is the country's only campus-based, student-staffed book publishing company. Directed by professors and industry professionals, it is a nonprofit activity of the Communication Department at Loyola University Maryland.

Using state-of-the-art technology and an experiential learning model of education, Apprentice House publishes books in untraditional ways. This dual responsibility as publishers and educators creates an unprecedented collaborative environment among faculty and students, while teaching tomorrow's editors, designers, and marketers.

Outside of class, progress on book projects is carried forth by the AH Book Publishing Club, a co-curricular campus organization supported by Loyola University Maryland's Office of Student Activities.

Eclectic and provocative, Apprentice House titles intend to entertain as well as spark dialogue on a variety of topics. Financial contributions to sustain the press's work are welcomed. Contributions are tax deductible to the fullest extent allowed by the IRS.

To learn more about Apprentice House books or to obtain submission guidelines, please visit www.apprenticehouse.com.

Apprentice House
Communication Department
Loyola University Maryland
4501 N. Charles Street
Baltimore, MD 21210
Ph: 410-617-5265 • Fax: 410-617-2198
info@apprenticehouse.com • www.apprenticehouse.com

CPSIA information can be obtained at www.ICGtesting.com
Printed in the USA
BVOW08s0443300716

457133BV00003B/5/P